DJUSD
Public Schools
Library Protection Act 1998

Wilson's Junior High School,
July 199

LIGHTNING TIME

by Douglas Rees

PUFFIN BOOKS

PUFFIN BOOKS
Published by the Penguin Group
Penguin Putnam Books for Young Readers,
345 Hudson Street, New York, New York 10014, U.S.A.
Penguin Books Ltd, 27 Wrights Lane, London W8 5TZ, England
Penguin Books Australia Ltd, Ringwood, Victoria, Australia
Penguin Books Canada Ltd, 10 Alcorn Avenue, Toronto, Ontario, Canada M4V 3B2
Penguin Books (N.Z.) Ltd, 182-190 Wairau Road, Auckland 10, New Zealand

Penguin Books Ltd, Registered Offices: Harmondsworth, Middlesex, England

First published in the United States of America by DK Publishing Inc., 1997
Published by Puffin Books,
a member of Penguin Putnam Books for Young Readers, 1999

1 3 5 7 9 10 8 6 4 2

LIBRARY OF CONGRESS CATALOGING-IN-PUBLICATION DATA
Rees, Douglas.
Lightning time / Douglas Rees.
p. cm.
Summary: Fourteen-year-old Theodore Worth struggles with the decision
to leave his home in Boston and join the controversial abolitionist
John Brown in the fight against slavery.
ISBN 0-14-130317-4
1. Brown, John, 1800–1859—Juvenile fiction. [1. Brown, John, 1800–1859—Fiction.
2. Abolitionists—Fiction. 3. Slavery—Fiction.
4. Afro-Americans—Fiction.] I. Title.
PZ7.R25475Li 1999 [Fic]—dc21 98-28615 CIP AC

Printed in the United States of America

To Dennise,

book aunt

CONTENTS

PART ONE

A Man of Many Names

ONE

Winter was mounting one last attack on Boston, an army of small, hard flakes that melted when they hit the ground. The road to Concord was a swamp of ice and mud. The horses threw up clumps of the stuff against the underside of our cab, and our wheels were covered to the hubs with it. There was a crackling crunch as our carriage lurched through another patch of rotten ice and into the rut below. The coach tipped crazily, and my mother, my father, and I were all jerked out of our seats.

The coachman got down from his perch and rapped on the door with his whip. "Excuse me, gents, you'll have to help me," he said.

"What is the problem?" my father replied, though that seemed obvious enough to me.

"The horses need a little help."

Grumbling, my father got down from the coach. I jumped out after him.

The front wheels were half-buried in a trench of mud.

"It appears to me you could have gone around this," my father said.

"Yep," the coachman agreed. "Now, here's what I need you to do. Each grab a spoke and pull backwards. This ain't a bad hole, and Dolly and Bill will have us out of it in a minute if you bear a hand. Then, I promise you, sir, we will drive around it."

Swearing under his breath, my father took off his coat and laid hands on a muddy spoke. I went to the other side and gripped mine. The coachman jumped back into his seat and cracked his whip over Bill's and Dolly's heads.

"Now, heave!" the coachman cried.

We heaved. The coach didn't budge.

"Again!" shouted the coachman. "Put your backs into it."

I pulled with all my strength but felt my feet sliding out from under me. I stumbled, caught myself, and heaved again. There was a sucking sound, the wheel turned, and I rolled down with it into the mud. The horses' rear hooves threw more muck as I lay there, splattering me on the only clean places left.

I got up laughing and trying to brush myself off. I looked at my father. He was as muddy as I was. Unlike me, he wasn't laughing. "Not an ideal night to go to a lecture, is it?" I said.

"Come along, gents, it's getting late," the coachman urged.

"Indeed it is not, Theodore," my father snapped. "And we are not going. Turn this cab around, sir," he called to the coachman.

"But Father, we're almost there," I said.

"That is enough, Theodore," my father said.

My mother leaned out of the cab. "Thee are angry,

my love," she said soothingly, "but we must go to the lecture, even as we are."

Mother was a Quaker and still spoke in the old-fashioned way, using "thee" with everyone but God. It was thanks to her that I was there at all, instead of at home with Amy and Talitha, my seven-year-old sisters, and an unwritable Latin composition.

"If we go into the Concord Congregational Church looking like this, we will become a topic of gossip all over Boston," my father said.

"My dear, what people may say does not matter," my mother told him. "What we do does. Thy great-grandfather was at Bunker Hill. Was not he dirty by the end of the day?"

"So was everyone else," my father growled.

"Many people are coming tonight. Many will have walked," my mother said. "And many who came in carriages may also have had to get out and push them. Please, my love. It means much to me."

"Which way would you like to go, sir?" the coachman called down.

"Please, dearest," my mother said.

"Concord," my father called to the coachman.

My mother smiled. "Thee will be glad, Hale," she said. "What we hear tonight will be important."

"Caroline, my love, I deplore what is happening in Kansas Territory as much as any man in Boston," Father said. "But I am not sure that what happens out there matters to Massachusetts."

My parents were at it again, arguing in their politest way over slavery. It was almost all they ever argued about. They adored each other and seemed to agree on everything else. They even said they agreed on slavery. But when it came down to what to do about it, they went around and around and got nowhere. As for me, I was curious. All I knew was what I'd been told, which was what everyone knew.

Once, slavery had been found only south of the Mason-Dixon Line. Then an exception had been made for Missouri. Massachusetts then gave up Maine to raise the number of free states. After that, the number of free and slave states was kept equal. That had been the "Missouri Compromise." It had stood for forty years. Then several new free states came into the Union. The South demanded, and got, a new policy. They insisted that the voters in each state should decide the slave question for themselves. Kansas was the first test of that policy.

Now North and South were each sending armed men there to insure that the new state would be their kind. War had begun last year, and now, in 1857, Americans were still killing each other in "Bleeding Kansas." This was what we were seeking to learn more about. I was glad to be going. Our speaker had taken part in the fighting. It ought to be exciting.

We lurched into Concord at last, and the ruts widened into cobblestoned streets. We clattered up to the doors of the Congregational Church.

There were several other carriages there, and many people hurrying to the church on foot. They were nearly as muddy as we were. Clearly they must have thought that what happened in Kansas mattered to Massachusetts.

My father cheered up a little when he saw so many others in our condition. "Perhaps I ought to go about like this more often," he said. "Looking as I do, no one with a manuscript under his arm would be likely to approach me."

My father was a publisher, and writers often sought him out. His firm, Worth House, was small but well thought of. He published novels mostly, but they were good books. No one looked down on my father for specializing in fiction.

As we shouldered into the church, a tall, sharp-nosed man with a black beard forced his way down the aisle toward us.

"Hello, Hale. I want a word with you in private," he said.

"About what, Mr. Howe?" my father replied as formally as possible. Although my mother and Julia Ward Howe were friends, my father never addressed her husband as anything but "Mister." Dr. Joshua Gridley Howe had been knighted a chevalier by the king of Greece and liked to be called "Chev," but my father refused to do it. "If 'Mister' was good enough for George Washington," he told me once, "it ought to be good enough for Howe."

"As I said, it is a private matter," Dr. Howe repeated.

"Perhaps after the lecture," my father said. "At the moment I am occupied in trying to find three seats together."

"Right this way," insisted Dr. Howe. "I took the liberty of keeping some seats in the front in hopes that you would be coming."

"Indeed," said my father.

But my mother smiled. "We thank thee, Dr. Howe."

He led us up to the front of the church. Mrs. Howe and my mother embraced, as they always did.

When we were seated, I couldn't help looking at the people around us. Nearly everyone who was known for anything in Boston or Concord was there.

Just behind us were Theodore Parker and Bronson Alcott and his family. Alcott, a believer in women's rights, had brought his wife and all his daughters. Mr. Emerson was there with his handyman, Henry Thoreau. Just in front of them were the Reverend Thomas Wentworth Higginson and a man I didn't recognize.

The man soon rose to speak. "Good evening, ladies and gentlemen," he said. "My name is Franklin Benjamin Sanborn. As many of you know, I conduct a school here in Concord. And I am an abolitionist."

There was a scattering of applause when he said this.

"The man whom I am about to introduce to you is also an abolitionist, a far greater one than I. For he has put his principles to the test in the fiery furnace of battle on the windy plains of Kansas. Neither the man nor the principles have been found wanting." Mr. Sanborn brought his fist down on the lectern.

This time the applause was louder.

"I am not free to name this man, though he is known now across the country. There is a price on his head. Our government wants him for crimes it says he has committed, crimes that were carried out in the name of liberty. There may be agents of that government among us tonight, ready to seize him. For that is what it has come to in the land of the free and the home of the brave, my fellow citizens. It has become a crime to fight for liberty. Thus, ladies and gentlemen, I have the honor to introduce to you a criminal. A man without a name. Almost, a man without a country. A wanted man. A hunted man. A patriot and a freedom fighter. A captain of men like himself. Ladies and gentlemen, I give you—"

And Mr. Sanborn sat down.

A few people clapped uncertainly.

In that moment of confusion, a tall, thin, gray man with a fierce jaw strode out from the back of the church to stand before the pulpit. His black suit was worn. His pants were stuffed into high boots that had seen a lot of travel. He looked us over slowly with sharp, dangerous eyes.

"My name is John Brown," he said. His voice was deep, his accent pure old-fashioned Yankee. With his granite face and his broad vowels, he might have been anyone's great-grandfather come back from the dead to address us.

"Praise be to God for the avenging of Israel," a woman called from the back.

Brown put up his hand. "Is there anyone here who would like to arrest me? I am worth two hundred fifty dollars to you."

I looked around. No one moved.

"As my friend Mr. Sanborn says, I am lately come from Kansas. I have done some fighting out there. I mean to go back and fight again. That is why I am here with you tonight. To ask your help for the next campaign. I imagine all of you know that there are really two Kansases now. There is a free Kansas, with its capital at Lawrence, and a slave Kansas, with its capital at Lecompton. The free Kansas is being settled by your friends and neighbors from New England and Ohio. The other is being settled by packs of slavery-loving ruffians and murderers from Missouri and Alabama."

He went on to tell us how his sons had gone out to Kansas Territory first, with fruit saplings and seeds. They had settled farms along Pottawatomie Creek.

But the Border Ruffians from Missouri had kept threatening them, trying to force them to leave. The Missourians didn't intend to stay in Kansas. They were there to make sure that Yankees didn't stay either.

Armed companies of Southerners came in from other states. Finally, some of them from Lecompton marched up to Lawrence and burned it to the ground. They destroyed everything, even the big stone hotel, which had been built to serve as a fortress. Brown, his sons, and their militia company had been marching to save the town but had arrived one day too late.

"And as we stood on that hill and looked at that twisting smoke and those still-rising flames, a messenger arrived. He told us that on the day Lawrence was burned, your own senator, Charles Sumner, had been beaten nearly to death with a cane by a Southern congressman who didn't care for what he had to say about slavery."

A shudder ran through the crowd. Sumner was still not recovered from the attack. And the Southern congressman had received hundreds of canes to replace the one he had broken across our senator's back. The South approved of such behavior. All New England believed it.

"From that time, from that place, I have been an active-duty soldier in the fight for freedom and Kansas," Brown said.

He came a step closer to us and held out his half-opened hands. He looked from one to the other. "Now the one thing all agree on is that two Kansases are too many. We and the South each reckon that there shall be only one. The question is, shall it be the free Kansas or the slave?"

"Free! Free!" some of the people shouted.

Brown put up a hand again. "I wish I could tell you that it will be so," he said. "But it may very well not be so. The Southern slavery men understand as well as we do what is at stake. Not only the future of Kansas, my friends, but the future of our entire republic. Under the government's policy, each new state is likely to become another Kansas. The old promise that slavery would be confined below the Mason-Dixon Line is dead. The slaver insists on his right to take what he considers to be his property—that is to say, another human being—into any state in the Union. He claims the right to pursue that property wherever in this land it may attempt to flee from him, and to compel anyone to help him do it. And the Congress of the United States has agreed that he has those rights. That is why there is war now in Kansas."

All around me, people were shifting in their seats. They were murmuring in agreement. One man across the aisle stood up, opened his mouth, clenched his fists, and sat down again.

"Now I have not told you anything you do not already know," Brown said. "The Fugitive Slave Act and the Kansas-Nebraska Act have been law for some time. I am only here to point out that if you do not agree with these laws, you must do something to oppose them."

"Tell us, tell us!"

My father harrumphed and crossed his arms over his chest.

"I do not ask you to return with me to Kansas and

fight," Brown said, looking straight at Father. "There are men enough for that. I have five sons waiting for me there—"

We broke into applause.

"—and we have friends enough to do the job. What we need is money for good weapons. In a few more weeks, it will be spring on the prairies again. The fighting will likely start early. Will you not, for the sake of a free Kansas, for a free country, for the sake of the slave yearning for freedom, give what you can?"

The man who had stood up before now rose again. He waved his tall hat over his head and shouted, "I propose we fill this hat with money unless someone here has a bigger one."

There were cheers and applause. The hat started bobbing up and down the pews while people sang hymns and talked.

When it finally reached us, my father took the hat and handed it on immediately.

"One moment, please, Hale," my mother said. She reached into her reticule and took out a silver dollar. I was amazed. Mother's reverence for thrift was profound. Brown must have touched her deeply. I felt in my pocket and found fifteen cents. It was all the money I had for the rest of the week, but I thought of the widow in the Bible who gave all she had, and put it in proudly. I was surprised to see that, although the hat was so heavy it was nearly falling apart, most of the money was nickels, dimes, and pennies.

The hat made its way up past Mr. Emerson and Mr. Thoreau and into the hands of Mr. Sanborn.

"Thank you, thank you, my friends!" Mr. Sanborn

shouted. "This money shall be consecrated to the liberty of man and the honor of God."

"I thank you, my friends," Brown added.

People started singing hymns in different parts of the church. Gradually, they settled on one, and sang it over and over. It made no particular sense, but it was one everybody knew, and it gave release to our feelings.

> *Praise God, from Whom all blessings flow;*
> *Praise Him, all creatures here below;*
> *Praise Him above, ye Heavenly host,*
> *Praise Father, Son, and Holy Ghost.*

While we were singing, Brown disappeared.

People began to file out of the church. We waited with Dr. Howe. When the building was empty, he bent his head close to my father's.

"See here, Hale," Dr. Howe began. "Our friend has a problem. That federal marshal who's followed him here from Kansas is across the street. We need a place to put Brown up for a couple of days. Preferably with someone who is not known to be an active abolitionist. Will you do it?"

"No," my father replied.

"It would only be for a day or two," Dr. Howe said. "We have another house ready to take him. But we fear it may be being watched. We know yours is not."

"That can only mean, sir, that your people have been spying on us," Father snapped. "Thank you for your solicitude, but it was unnecessary. I will never give houseroom to an assassin."

Dr. Howe reddened. "John Brown is no assassin," he answered. "He is a Christian and a fighter for freedom."

"He murdered four men on Osawatomie Creek the night after he failed to save Lawrence, and the whole country knows it," my father replied. "Dragged them from their homes and butchered them with broadswords."

Dr. Howe glared at Father. His jaws worked. At last he said, "There is no proof of that, Worth."

"And what is your marshal waiting to arrest him for if not those murders?" my father said quietly.

"That's true," said a voice behind us.

Father and I turned.

"I am wanted for murder in Kansas. I understand that the charge is not quite accurate, since I did not kill anybody that night myself. But I organized the killing. And I put one bullet into one man to make sure he was dead. Which he was." John Brown turned to Dr. Howe. "It is all right, Chev," he said. "Any place will do for me tonight. It doesn't matter so much, since I won't be taken alive in any case."

Now my mother was standing beside us, her hand in my father's.

"But what had these men done, Mr. Brown?" she asked.

"Done?" Brown said, smiling at her. "Not much. Only threatened other folks who lived along the creek. They promised to kill some Free-Soilers who had the bad sense to live nearby. One old man ran away and froze to death on the prairie because he knew they meant what they said. But I don't reckon there's any great crime in that. The murder of an abolitionist is no crime in Kansas. Had those four men I ordered killed come and killed me instead, there'd be no federal marshal after them."

"But why those four, sir?" my mother insisted.

"Well, ma'am," Brown drawled, "after the slavers

burned Lawrence, I was mighty hot to get back at them any way I could. Those men were well known in our district. I reckoned killing them would have a good effect."

"The effect it seems to have had is to turn Kansas into a war ground," my father said.

"That is so, sir," said Brown. "But I do not apologize for my part in it, since we fight for freedom against slavery. What I did forced every man to choose his side."

"I think our government's policy in Kansas is a scandal," my father said. "I despise its weakness. But I think you seek to split this country in two over slavery. I can never agree to that."

"And what do you propose instead?" Brown asked.

"I detest slavery as much as any man in Boston," my father replied. "But if you destroy the Union, the South will still have its slaves. It is only within the Union that the abolitionist has any hope of victory."

"And what hope is that?" Brown said. "Tell me, sir. I am anxious to know. I have a wife and children I yearn to go home to. If there is some hope of freeing the slaves without fighting, I want to know about it. What hope do you see?"

My father was silent.

"You may be right, sir," Brown agreed. "Perhaps it is better to live in a country where the slaveholder has all the rights and the free man none. I can only say that I have heard the cry of the slave in his chains and it has pierced my heart. This being so, I can only follow my conscience where it leads me. And it has led me to war."

Everyone was silent then.

Mother put her hand on my father's arm. "I believe we should take him in, Hale," she said.

"Indeed?" said my father.

Dr. Howe stared. He was known to be a supporter of women's rights, but he was no more used to seeing a wife disagree in public with her husband than most people.

"If we turn him away and he is captured tonight, then everything that follows from that will be our doing. If we keep him safe for a night or two, we have done our part to preserve his life. That, I think, is our duty." My father started to speak, but my mother went on. "Thee are right, my love, but so is Mr. Brown. He is wanted for his part in murders. But specifically for his part in murdering slavery men. Thee and I know that this is true. Thee say that thee hate slavery, and I know that this is true. Do thee hate it enough to risk something for thy beliefs?"

"I won't risk you and the children for anything," my father said.

"I want to help," I blurted out. "He can have the spare room, after all."

"This is not your decision, Theodore," my father snapped, but my mother said, "And I will answer for Talitha and Amy, as well as myself."

"And if this marshal comes to our door with his warrant and enters our house and Mr. Brown makes good his promise to kill or be killed—" my father began.

"We must pray it will not come to that," my mother replied.

Father stood with his fists clenched like stones for a moment. Then he turned to Dr. Howe. "We are leaving," he said. "We will be home within two hours. Bring him to the back door after that time."

"Not I," said Dr. Howe. "Mr. Sanborn will convey Mr. Brown tonight."

"I thank you, sir," Brown said.

"I do not thank you, Mr. Brown," my father declared. "But you will be as safe as we can make you."

"It will be an honor, sir," I said, ignoring my father's scowl.

And as quickly as that, we, my own ordinary family, were suddenly doing something exciting. I hoped Brown would tell us some war stories.

On the street, our carriage was standing by itself, the horses drowsing under their blankets.

My father jerked open the cab door. The driver was asleep in one corner, wrapped in his cape.

"We are leaving, sir," Father nearly shouted.

"Right," sighed the coachman, stumbling out past us. I smelled whiskey on his breath.

"This night—" my father grumbled.

The coachman tried to climb into his box but slipped. I went to steady him.

"Thanks, boy," he said with an amiable grin. "Want to ride up with me?"

I agreed at once.

"Theodore, come down," my father ordered.

I bent as close as I could to his face. "I think I'd better," I said. "He's been drinking—"

"I know that, Theodore."

"—and up here I can watch for any more large holes. We don't want to get stuck again."

My father thought that over. "Very well. See that we do not," he said, and climbed into the cab with Mother.

The coachman took the reins and got us back onto the muddy road to Boston. Then he settled down into his cape and pulled his hat over his eyes.

"Sir—" I said.

"Nothing to worry about. Dolly and Bill know the way home. Just wake me up when we get back to pavement." He pulled a bottle out of his coat and offered it to me.

"Oh, no thanks," I said, feeling flustered.

The coachman winked at me, took a long swig, and closed his eyes with a happy sigh.

"'This night,'" Father had said in disgust. It seemed like a fine one to me. Before we left Boston, my mother had said, "Theodore is fourteen, Hale, and should hear this lecture. He is old enough to begin taking part in the country's business. Even when it is bad business. Perhaps he can help better it." Now, suddenly, I was a part of it.

I picked up the reins that had fallen from the coachman's slack hands. I liked the feel of them in mine.

TWO

"We must refer to him as Hawkins. Nelson Hawkins," my father said. "Howe whispered it to me as we were leaving."

The three of us were standing in the kitchen, looking into the backyard. The room was dark except for the low orange glow of our iron stove. I could hardly see my parents. They stood facing each other, shadows against the windows.

"He will be safe here, Hale," my mother said, touching Father's shoulder.

"Safe," my father repeated. "May we all be."

Our maid, Mary, put her head in at the door. "I've got the room ready, ma'am," she said.

"Thank thee, Mary, for thy trouble," my mother said. "Please set one more place at breakfast tomorrow."

Mary nodded, spun on her heel, and marched out. She didn't approve of guests at this time of night. If she had known what kind of man was coming, she would have approved even less.

"Will thee want anything else?" my mother asked.

"No, thank you," my father said.

"I will say good night, then."

"We shall be very quiet when he comes, I assure you," he replied as my mother slipped out of the room.

The storm was rising. A stinging cloud of snow galloped south now, blown by a shrieking wind. The barren branches of our oak trees clawed at the sky. I had the fancy that they'd torn down the stars.

"You may go to bed also, Theodore," my father said.

"No, sir," I said, "I want to stay with you."

"Well," my father said after a moment, "I suppose you are in no more danger downstairs than upstairs."

I moved closer to him. It was strange. I was in our own kitchen, in the house where I had spent all my life so far. But now everything seemed different; precarious and vulnerable. It was the other side of excitement.

The wind blew; the house groaned a little. My father and I waited. At last, I saw two dim shapes detach themselves from the dark and come slowly toward the door. There was a quiet knock.

I picked up the fire poker. "Just in case our visitors are not whom we expect," I said.

"And what good will that do if they are not, Theodore?" my father asked, and opened the door.

I heard Mr. Sanborn's voice. "Have I the honor of addressing Mr. Hale Worth?"

My father agreed that he did.

"Permit me. I am Franklin Benjamin Sanborn. This is Mr. 'Nelson Hawkins.'" I could hear the quotation marks around the name.

"Come in, gentlemen," my father said.

I put down the poker.

"It is all right, sir," Mr. Brown said. "We weren't followed."

We all shook hands, and my father introduced me.

"How d'ye do, young man?" Brown said to me.

"Very well, thank you, sir."

Mr. Sanborn turned back to the door. "I must go. Mr. Hawkins will require your hospitality for only two or three days. We have his next refuge arranged for, as soon as we are sure that no one is watching it."

"So I understood," my father said.

"I will bid you good night, then," Mr. Sanborn said. I let him out.

Here in our kitchen, John Brown, in snow-pelted black coat and broad-brimmed hat, carpetbag in one hand, seemed more a part of the night than ever.

"Would you care to go to bed, Mr. Hawkins?" Father asked, lighting a candle.

"Yes, thanks," Brown said. He followed my father to the stairs.

"May I take your bag, Mr. Hawkins?" I offered.

He handed it to me. It was surprisingly heavy. "Take care with it, young man. If you set it down hard, it might go off," he said.

Intrigued and a little frightened, I followed them up the stairs and down the hall.

I lowered the bag softly onto the bed in the room next to mine.

"Will you need anything else tonight?" my father asked.

"Nothing," Brown told him. "I thank you again for giving hospitality to a wanted man."

"We breakfast at seven," my father said. "Good night."

He and I left the room. I heard Brown turning the key in the lock behind us.

I undressed quickly and pulled my cold flannel nightshirt on as fast as I could. My bed was like ice, and as I lay curled into a ball while my body slowly warmed it, I heard a series of thumps and scrapes come from Brown's room. He was moving the furniture. I could tell exactly what he was doing by the sounds. First he pushed the bureau against the door. Then he shoved the bed against the bureau.

The racket wakened Amy and Talitha in their room across the hall. "Marmy," they called. "Marmy, what is that noise?"

I went in to them, shivering.

They were sitting up in bed, looking like frightened owls.

"Hush," I whispered. "It's only Mr. Hawkins getting settled."

"Who is Mr. Hawkins, Theodore?" Talitha asked.

"A man who will be staying with us for a few days."

"Why, is he a friend?" Amy asked. She pulled the blankets up higher under her chin.

"Yes. A very great friend," I said. "But don't tell anyone at school that we have a guest."

"Why not?"

"Because it would be impolite." That was a good answer for Amy. She was very concerned these days with what was polite and what was not. This was especially true when she could accuse someone else of impoliteness.

But Talitha said, "When aunts and uncles come to visit, we tell everyone. That's not impolite, is it?"

"No," I told her. "But Mr. Hawkins is different. He is not a relative, you see. So just be careful to say nothing about him, or the other girls will laugh at you behind your backs for not knowing better."

"Why is he moving our furniture?" Talitha wanted to know.

"Mr. Hawkins is not from Boston," I said. "Where he comes from, they arrange furniture differently."

"But he's pushing things up against the door," Amy pointed out.

"Mr. Hawkins has been living in the West," I said. "Where he is from there are bears."

"No bears around Boston, Theodore," Talitha said wisely.

"Well, perhaps he can't get used to a place without bears."

"I think you are making up a story," Talitha replied.

"You're right," I said. "I'm only guessing about Mr. Hawkins. Let's ask him tomorrow."

That satisfied them. They lay down and allowed me to tuck them in.

I got back into my own bed, but I couldn't sleep.

There were no bears in Boston, but there was a federal marshal who wanted the man I had called Hawkins. There was a price on our visitor's head. The national government had put it there. And he thought the threat was real enough that he had barricaded his room.

I lay awake remembering what my father had feared. I imagined the marshal, a thick, ugly man with two

Colt's revolvers in his belt and a shotgun. He had a squad of our Boston police behind him. When Mary opened the door, he thumbed his badge at her and pushed his way in.

My mother was standing in the mudroom, blocking his way to the rest of the house. She barely came up to his shoulder. "What does thee mean to invade my house this way?" she demanded.

The police sergeant took off his cap and said, "Begging your pardon, ma'am, but we're here on most official business."

"Not official enough," I said, coming to stand beside Mother. "You have no warrant."

The marshal yanked a paper out of his coat pocket and thrust it forward. "Here you are, boy. A warrant for the arrest of John Brown, also known as Nelson Hawkins. Wanted for murder in Kansas, as I expect you know. Now stand aside."

What would I do at this point? What could we do in the face of guns, police, the power of the government?

Suppose I tried to block the marshal from going up the stairs? Would he shoot me? And what would John Brown do? Would he attempt to escape, or would he appear at the landing with weapons in his hands, blazing at the marshal and police? What would happen to us then?

The wind struck the house a sudden blow and I jumped.

I had known since I was old enough to understand that there were great winds in the world. Men struggled over mighty questions like independence, abolition, and democracy, and these struggles made history. Tonight I had learned that there were dark things deeper than the winds that flowed in secret and came to light only a little. And they were as fierce as any storm.

Now these things were trying to get into my house. No, they had got in. Something deep and dark was in the next room, and its enemies were seeking it. And I greatly suspected that none of these things cared much what happened to one man and his wife, two little girls and a boy.

It was hours before I slept.

THREE

 I woke to the sound of the furniture in the next room being moved again. The light came in through my windows clear and gray. Feeling very tired, I rolled out of bed and dressed. I met John Brown on the landing.

"Good morning, young man," he said.

"Good morning, Mr. Hawkins," I replied.

He was dressed as he had been the night before. I spied the butts of two revolvers sticking out of his boot tops. When he saw that I had noticed them, he smiled and shoved them out of sight. Then we went down to breakfast.

Mary had laid on a company meal, with plenty of ham and eggs, as well as fresh bread and fruit. We were the last ones at the table. My father introduced Mr. Hawkins to Talitha and Amy. I sat down. John Brown remained standing.

"I beg your pardon, Mr. Worth," he said after a minute. "Have you already said the grace?"

My father led grace at dinners. We rarely said it any other time.

"Would you be so good as to lead us, Mr. Hawkins?" he said.

John Brown turned his chair around backwards and tilted it toward himself. He leaned his arms on the back of the chair and prayed, "Lord, bless this food to our health and Your service. Bless our work, and grant that we may recollect to thank You for it in the business of the day. Above all, bless this family, and my own. Keep all the children safe, and make them good. Grant that this day may bring us all one step closer to that Heavenly City where we may dwell forever in Your presence. Amen."

"Amen," we all agreed.

John Brown turned his chair back around and sat down.

"Are you frightened of bears, Mr. Hawkins?" Talitha asked.

"Somewhat," Brown said. "Have you got many bears in these parts?"

"No," said Amy. "So you don't have to push the furniture against the door at night."

Then John Brown did something I thought he would never do. He laughed. His whole body shook, but he never made a sound. Finally, he said, "I am very relieved to hear it, child. But I rather suspect one or two large bears may have followed me from Kansas. So perhaps I had better do it anyway, for those Kansas bears make a terrible mess, and I shouldn't like them to spoil your mother's pretty little room."

Then he turned to my father. "I had no opportunity of saying so last night, Mr. Worth, but I greatly admire a book you published two years ago. *Stilicho; or, The Barbarian of Rome.* I read it through three times."

"I fear you were the only one who read it at all," Father

said. "Sales were disappointing. Still, I am pleased to hear that you enjoyed it. I will inform the author if you like."

"A very improving novel," Brown said. "It is a great pity that more people did not see the value in the book."

"That is the way with most novels," my father observed.

"Most novels are not of such a quality," Brown replied.

My father put down his fork. "Tell me what you found so praiseworthy," he said.

"Stilicho is a great warrior who tries to save Rome by compromising his principles, but he fails; he is poisoned, and the barbarians overwhelm the empire," Brown said. "*Stilicho* teaches us not to compromise."

"I don't believe that was the meaning the author intended," Father said. "Nor is it what I saw in the book when I edited it. We saw it as Stilicho's undoing by his own pride. Had he remained loyal to the government he had sworn to defend, he might have lived. He would, at least, have kept his honor."

"Then I suggest the author did not completely understand his own work," Brown said. "Stilicho's tragedy is that there is no longer anyone worthy of his loyalty."

My father poured himself another cup of coffee. "Frankly, Mr. Hawkins, I had not thought of you as a great reader."

"I mostly read books on scientific farming, military subjects, and religion, but I am very fond of any improving literature I can get," Brown replied. "When I lived in Ohio, I kept a library and a boarding school in my home for a time."

"Really," my father remarked. I could tell Brown had surprised him.

"And did thee teach girls, or only boys in thy school?" Mother asked.

"Only boys for pay, since it was a boarding school and there was no room for girls," Brown told her. "But I have taught my own daughters somewhat."

"Do little girls not have to go to school in Ohio?" Amy asked.

"It was a rough, new place then," Brown said. "I hope there are schools for them now."

"Remember thy grandparents live in Cincinnati, Amy," my mother said. "And it is a fine, modern city with many schools."

"Oh," said Amy, losing interest in Ohio.

"Do you have many little girls?" Talitha asked.

"God has given me twenty children, though he has taken some of them back to Heaven," Brown said.

"Thee did not mention any daughters in thy talk last night, Mr. Hawkins," my mother remarked. "Are any of them in Kansas?"

"All are at my farm in New York State, ma'am," Brown said. "I hope to visit them before I go west again."

"Why did you turn the chair around to say grace?" Talitha asked.

"It's an old custom of the Scots Presbyterians," Brown explained. "When there is no pulpit, a man makes his own. I favor the practice, though I am a Congregationalist myself."

"We are Friends," Amy informed him, using the proper, formal word for the Quakers. "All except Father."

"I greatly admire the Friends," Brown said. "They were the first church to call slavery wrong, a hundred years ago. I wish all churches thought so."

"Friends also believe that war is wrong," I said, wondering what response I might get.

Brown fixed me with his dark eyes. "War is wrong. Slavery is wrong. On these points the Friends and I agree," he said. "We disagree only on which of them is the more wrong."

Father passed the bread around the table. I offered Brown the butter.

"No, thank you," he said. "Have you any molasses?"

I handed him that. We all watched as he sliced off a great wedge of bread and smothered it in thick brown molasses.

"Is that how people eat bread in Kansas?" Amy asked.

"I have eaten bread this way since I was a boy," Brown told her. "But I have eaten stranger things than this in Kansas."

"What sorts of things?" Talitha asked.

"Oh, skunk drumsticks, snapping turtle soup, rattlesnake pie when I can get it. It's mighty good with fried grasshoppers mixed in." Brown's eyes were twinkling.

"Did you ever eat a lion?" Talitha asked wonderingly.

"Only a little one," Brown said.

"But there ain't no lions out West," Amy exclaimed.

"There are mountain lions," I offered.

"I reckon it was one of those," Brown said. "There was a small mountain close by."

"But little girls in Kansas don't eat rattlesnakes, do they?" Talitha asked.

"Oh, no," Brown said. "Little girls are too delicate for that. A Kansas girl has to be ten years old before she's allowed to eat rattlesnake."

Talitha squealed.

Amy said, "But do they put molasses on their bread?"

"No," said Brown. "I believe they don't."

"Then I don't believe they eat rattlesnakes, either."

"Well, child," Brown said, "you never did ask me if they put molasses on their rattlesnakes."

"Now I know you are telling a story," Amy said, in such a way that all of us laughed.

"You have caught me, child," Brown said, once he had stopped his silent shaking. "But I have eaten some mighty strange things in Kansas."

When breakfast was over, the girls and I got up to start for school. But my mother said, "How would thee children like to stay home today?"

Father gave her an odd look yet said nothing. The girls yelped with delight. I looked out the window at the cold, gray sky and the thin coat of icy snow and smiled. If Brown's presence would keep me away from Mr. Weems's School for Boys, he could stay for a year.

"I, in any case, must go in to the office," Father announced.

"Of course thee must, Hale."

Then I understood. Mother was afraid that the girls had liked Mr. Brown too well. They might go to school and tell their friends about our visitor. But how could she think that I would be so foolish?

Father put on his coat and left. He had a long, cold walk to the shop on Chester Street. I watched him hunch into the wind and set off down our hill, leaving the family he didn't want to leave, going into work as if everything was normal, because that was the best way to help a man he did not want to help.

After he left, the rest of us went into the back parlor.

"Have you any chores that I might do for you, Mrs. Worth?" Brown asked. "I don't love to be idle."

"Thank thee, Mr. Hawkins," my mother replied. "But we have a man who comes. Perhaps thee could keep company with the children this morning while he is here. He does not come into the house."

"I would be pleased," Brown said.

Now it came to me why I was being kept home. My mother did not want to entertain a strange man while her husband was away. I was standing in for my father. I liked the feeling.

And so my sisters and mother and I passed the morning in the back parlor playing children's games with John Brown. His hair was iron gray and his skin was deeply wrinkled, but I have seen few men who were spryer or stronger. After we had played puss-in-the-corner and ring-around-the-rosy and everything else the girls knew, he and I took them on our backs and played horses. Afterwards, he bounced them on his knee together and sang to them.

What he did at the end of the morning was hard to believe, even seeing it. He had Amy and Talitha each stand on one of his hands and lifted them up toward the ceiling. Watching, my mother gasped and covered her mouth, but the girls cooed. John Brown held his arms straight out from his sides. They barely trembled. "Some day, little girls, you can tell people that J— Mr. Nelson Hawkins did this with you," he said.

He set them down slowly.

That afternoon, when the girls had been sent upstairs for naps, Mother, Brown, and I returned to the parlor. Mother asked if he wanted coffee. He asked for tea. When Mary had brought it, he carefully removed his two big pistols from his boots and laid the weapons out beside the tea things. Slowly, as Mother watched in silence, he pulled a smaller pistol from his pants. He set out two knives along with them. Then he began to clean the weapons, one by one. He began with the knives, sharpening their edges with a small whetstone, then sliding them back into their scabbards. He set the small pistol's bullets in a straight row, then took it apart and cleaned it. When it was put back together and reloaded, he went on to the next, humming one of the hymns he'd sung to the girls. Finally, when he was working on the last pistol, he said, "I am glad to see that you aren't nervy, ma'am. Many women would object to a man cleaning his pistols in the parlor."

My mother said nothing.

"Oh, this is only the back parlor, Mr. Hawkins. You may do as you like here," I joked.

He smiled and snapped the cylinder of the revolver back into place. Then he held it out to me.

With a glance at my mother, I crossed the room and took it. It felt heavy, but not as heavy as I had expected. I didn't know how to hold it. I cocked the hammer and snapped the trigger. It had a good, crisp, hard sound.

"Have you ever held a pistol before?" Brown asked me.

"No," I admitted. At that moment it seemed as though I had been shirking my duty, as though I ought to have been carrying guns all my life.

"Let me show you something," Brown said. He stood, took the weapon from me, and held it out straight in front of him with both hands. He spread his feet wide apart. "This is the best stance for a pistol. In this position you can kill a man at fifty yards if you're good," he said. "But sometimes you are in too much of a hurry."

He handed it back to me, and I copied what he had done. Brown nodded. "Right smart."

My mother's face was grim. When I gave back the weapon, she let out her breath.

"Would you like to try it, Mrs. Worth?" Brown asked.

"No, thank thee," my mother said. "I have no love for carnal weapons."

"I felt so once," Brown replied. "Before I went to Kansas, I could never see the use of them. Now, carnal weapons and the money to get them are almost all I think about."

"Thee fight against an evil thing," my mother said. "I wish thee did not do it in so evil a way."

Brown stuffed his weapons back into his clothes as he spoke. "When I was a boy younger than your son, I used to drive cattle a hundred miles to sell to the army. That was back during the 1812 war. What I saw in the camps turned me against soldiering. Crime, corruption, and villainy was all the soldiering our militia knew. When I became a man, I never would serve. I paid the fine instead. But I have come to think there are some things a man must fight for."

"War is an evil thing always," Mother declared. "Persuasion is the only sure way to end slavery."

"I wish all men could be convinced so," Brown said. "But what remedy is there for those who will not be?"

"There are prayers," said my mother.

"I do pray for the end of slavery," Brown said. "And so, I know, do you, ma'am. And so, I'm sure, does every slave. But these millions of prayers rising to Heaven every day have not yet made one master free one soul from slavery, so far as I know."

"Killing leads only to more killing. As thee know well from experience," my mother said.

"That is so," Brown replied. "But my inner light shows me that slavery is a greater evil than war."

"Thy answers are so good, Mr. Hawkins, it is hard to remember that thee are wrong," my mother said.

Mary came into the room. "Beg pardon, but a message has come for Mr. Hawkins," she said, and handed him a folded sheet of paper.

"It's from Howe," Brown said. "They are sure now that my next hideout is safe. I will be leaving tonight."

"Will he be staying to dinner?" Mary asked.

"Yes," replied my mother.

"Thank you, ma'am," Brown said.

Mother stood up. "I must help Mary in the kitchen for a while," she told us. "Perhaps Mr. Hawkins would be interested to see thy telegraph, Theodore."

"Would you be, Mr. Hawkins?" I asked.

"I should be grateful," Brown said.

We went up to my room. I kept my telegrapher's key on a small table in the corner. It had no wires. I used it only to practice.

"Do you know the Morse code?" Brown asked.

"Yes, of course," I said. "And I even know a lot of the abbreviations and shortcuts real telegraphers use. Bob Gibbons down at the railroad station is teaching me."

"It's a fine thing to see a young man improve his mind with such useful knowledge," Brown said. "Do you mean to work at it when you're older?"

"Oh, no," I said. "This is only my hobby. My father doesn't like me to do it."

Brown looked surprised. "Why?" he asked.

"He thinks it's beneath me," I said. "He thinks I'll meet the wrong sort of people. And he wants me to spend more time studying for Harvard. He wants me to go there before I join him at Worth House."

"And what do you want?" Brown asked me.

His question surprised and flattered me. "Well ..." I shrugged. "I love books. And it's exciting to meet the people who write them. I suppose I will."

Brown stroked his chin. "Time is our most precious gift from the Almighty. We ought not to waste it," he said. "Your father is right about that. But I think you have made a fine choice of a hobby. A fine choice." He clicked the key up and down a couple of times. "When I was your age, this thing did not exist. Now it seems we cannot exist without it. A message flies from one end of the country to the next in seconds. Who could have imagined it? Lightning itself carries our thoughts now. Yes. Our times are lightning."

He turned back to me. "What do you think, young Worth? Are some things to be fought for?"

"I don't know," I replied.

"A man ought to have an opinion," Brown said.

"Then I shall think about it," I told him.

"The time is coming when we shall all need to know our minds," Brown went on. "It did not trouble your mother much when I cleaned my guns. It was when I handed one to you she became Quaker-minded."

I nodded.

"How did the pistol feel in your hand?" Brown asked.

"I liked it," I said.

"Then remember that feel, and remember the look on your mother's face," Brown said. "They will help you to decide."

"Is my father right?" I asked. "Do you want to start a civil war?"

"I am only one man," Brown said. "I cannot even raise the money to arm one company of men with good guns."

"Will there be much more fighting in Kansas come the spring?"

"I reckon so," Brown said. "Or if not in Kansas, somewhere else."

"Where?" I asked.

"It may be one place; it may be another. Every time a new state is added to the Union from now on, there will likely be a new war there. Maybe in the older states, too."

"Mr. Hawkins, I have something I want to give you," I said. I went over to a box on my bookcase. Inside was a five-dollar golden eagle my grandmother Evans had sent me for my last birthday. "This is for your work. I am sorry it is all I have."

"No one can give more than all."

"You might call me Theodore if you care to," I said.

"Then I thank you, Theodore," Brown said. He tapped the key again. "Could we not spend an hour or so at this key?" he asked. "I should like to learn a little."

So we spent the time until dinner in my room. I taught John Brown that day all he ever knew of the Morse code. By evening, when my father came home, he was tapping out his name, .————...—. —...—.———.———. , over and over.

Father arrived home with his mouth still set in a grim

line. It vanished when Mother told him that Brown would be leaving that night. Smiling, my father said, "I was able to locate a copy of *Stilicho* in the shop today, Mr. Hawkins, if you would care to have it."

"Indeed I would," Brown said. "My old copy is far away from here."

Every time the door to the kitchen opened, I caught the smell of my mother's spice cake. That was what she had been doing in the kitchen with Mary. I looked forward to dessert more than usual.

But dessert came and went and was not spice cake.

It was not until Mr. Sanborn arrived to take our visitor wherever he was going next that my mother brought the cake out. It was wrapped up for Brown alone.

"This is my best baking," she said. "I would not have thee leave my house remembering only the words that passed between us this afternoon."

"They were good words to hear, ma'am," Brown said. "I thank you for this cake, and for all besides. Including the words."

Talitha and Amy lined up to kiss him.

I shook his hand and said, "Good-bye, Mr. Hawkins. I will think about what you said."

"Good-bye, Theodore." Brown put his firm hand on my shoulder. Perhaps Chev Howe had felt the same when the king of Greece knighted him. "Thank you for teaching me to write my name in lightning. And for the other thing. It was a noble gift."

My father raised an eyebrow, and I explained: "Morse code."

My father handed two books to him. The first was *Stilicho*. The second was a small, handsome book from a set in his own library. *"Julius Caesar,"* my father said. "It is very informative on the fate of conspirators."

"Was not one of those conspirators 'the noblest Roman of them all'?" Brown remarked.

"Yes," my father replied. "He was called so because he fought to preserve his republic, not to destroy it."

"And he failed," Brown said. "The Roman republic lived by slavery. That's a bad thing for a republic to do, seemingly."

"The Roman republic fell, and the slaves were still slaves," my father said.

"Well, sir, your ideas and mine differ materially on what is best for our country," Brown said. "But I thank you for the book. I've never seen a better."

My father did not answer, but I felt the anger behind his silence. I could not understand it. John Brown was defending his country, not betraying it. Why couldn't he see that?

"We must be going," Mr. Sanborn said. "We are expected at Judge—excuse me. We are expected."

The two of them left by the back way. We watched until once again Brown became part of the night. The wind had shifted at sunset and was blowing warm again. I noticed that only Mr. Sanborn had left footprints in the melting snow. Even with no one after him, Brown had been careful where he stepped.

FOUR

Father was different for weeks after Brown's visit. It was as though, having let someone from outside into his careful life, even for one night, he was afraid something else might happen to upset it.

One evening, he came into my room. I was studying my geometry, trying to prove something pointless about the section of a cone. I looked up, grateful to be interrupted.

"Theodore, I have been thinking," he began. "I have decided that the time has come for you to put away your telegraph. I have given the matter careful consideration, not overlooking the fact that telegraphy is, in its way, useful knowledge. But your toying with it has gone on long enough. It is a skill you will never need, and it distracts you from what ought to be your real pursuits."

I flushed.

"I am sure I have your agreement."

"No," I said. I was not going to give up my key.

"The sort of people who engage in telegraphy, Theodore, are frequently disreputable and are never the sort of people with whom our sort associate. There is no point in continuing."

Our voices had started to rise, and brought my mother to the door. When she heard what the matter was, she took my part.

"We cannot keep Theodore at home forever," she said. "And he cannot spend all his time studying. As for telegraphers being persons of low worth, I think thee are wrong, my love. It is true they are poorly paid, but they are decent. Remember that this is one of the few things a woman may honestly do to support herself."

She had my father there. Like Dr. Howe, he was a strong believer in women's rights.

"This thing has done him no harm, and like any learning, it is good in itself," she went on. "Theodore should be allowed to continue."

My father paused, calculating his chances against Mother's arguments. Finally, he nodded. "Reluctantly, Theodore, reluctantly. And as long as your school marks remain acceptable."

My marks were always acceptable, if no more than that. Weems's school was exclusive, expensive, and run on the highest principles of dullness. Knowledge was presented in such a way as to mummify the brain in the shortest time possible. Mr. Weems intended to prepare us for Harvard or kill us. He seemed to feel that one end was as good as the other. I hated it there.

To be fair to Weems, the other students seemed not to mind, or even to notice. They were all from old Boston families like me. Unlike me, they were pure Boston, running back to its founding on both sides. I had a Quaker mother who had been born in New Jersey. This made me close to a foreigner. My classmates were not unfriendly, exactly. They simply preferred their own company.

But this was the place my father had chosen to send me to become a proper Bostonian. "I know that many of these boys lack your mind and spirit, Theodore," my father had told me. "But you must learn to get on with people like that. They will become the men among whom you will pass your life. The mere fact of your having been at school with them will be an advantage to you, whether you were popular or not. And as for Weems's dullness"— he shrugged—"school is supposed to be dull. You should not expect to be exempt from what every well-educated boy has suffered."

We heard from our abolitionist friends that Brown had not done well on his speaking tour. Everywhere he went, people had come to hear him and cheered what he had to say. They had promised thousands of dollars to his cause. But they had given him pennies. It seemed that my five dollars had been real money after all.

"Julia Ward Howe told me that he had over thirty thousand dollars in pledges when he left New England," my mother said. "But she believes he got only a tenth of what was promised."

"Three thousand dollars are three thousand too much for that man," Father snapped. "No sensible person would give him a nickel."

"I gave him a dollar," my mother said quietly.

"And you protected him. You gave him books," I protested.

"I gave him protection because my wife made me see that I must," he replied. "I gave him books that I thought might make him see his error. As for the man himself"— he measured his words out slowly—"he is dangerous and untrustworthy. He is a fanatic, with grandiose notions of himself. I confess that I should probably want John Brown for a neighbor if I were a frontiersman trying to raise a family in the wilderness. But it will take more than one old farmer with delusions of grandeur to end slavery in this country. He should leave these things to his betters."

"But his betters are doing nothing," I replied.

"Then it may be that there is nothing to be done."

Nothing to be done. In the months after John Brown hid in our house, I thought more than once, *We can put that on Father's tombstone. Here lies Hale Worth. Nothing to be done.*

The fall of 1857 came, and a financial panic, the worst in our history, crept across the country, closing businesses and throwing men out of work. Sales of Father's books fell to nearly nothing. Many other publishers went under. But nothing changed in my life except in measured, predictable ways, as my father expected. I ground out my days at Weems's school.

At least Father didn't try to interfere with my telegraphy again. Whenever I could after school, I slipped away to see my one good friend, Bob Gibbons, at the Western of Boston Railroad.

Bob had never told me where he came from, and I thought I should not ask. He'd never mentioned a family. He'd mentioned working in Baltimore and Brooklyn before Boston—"All the *B*'s. When I'm done with the *B* towns, I'll get onto the *C*'s. I'll never stay put. I know the inside of a barroom better than a schoolroom," he said with a laugh, "and I learned more there, that's for sure. Learned the Morse. If you can learn the Morse, you can learn anything you want to know. I can outfight any man my size and outtalk the rest. I haven't been afraid since I was nine years old, and I was wrong then. Been on my own since I was twelve, and I'll be on my own till the day I die.... They always need operators. I can pick up and go whenever I feel like it. That's what you call freedom."

I kept our friendship secret. I never brought him home. My father and mother would see Bob as a threat to their precious son.

I'd met Bob when I'd wandered into the depot looking for someone to teach me the Morse. He'd been rapping out messages with a little half-smile on his face and hadn't noticed me at first. When he did, he asked me my business in a friendly way. When I told him what I wanted, he'd tipped his hat back and said, "Sit down, buddy. Any guy can teach you the Morse, but nobody can teach you as well as I can. And you look smart. I bet you can teach me a few things, too."

He'd just arrived in Boston—"Blew in off the track and thought I'd sit down. Guess I'll stay till the wind blows hard enough to move me again." And we'd started teaching each other what we knew. "Listenin' to you is better than reading the books'd be, Ted. I can ask you just what I want to know. Don't have to bother with the rest of it."

I flattered myself that Bob hadn't been blown down the track again because he liked me. I hoped he'd never leave.

He was only about a year older than I was but had been a telegrapher for three. He walked fast and rolling everywhere he went. He spent his time at work, though, with his feet up on his desk and his eyes closed.

"Not sleeping, only just dozing. Eyes closed, ears open. Ever alert for the summons to action," he said.

That was true. When a message that concerned him clicked over the wires, he swung his feet down, reached for his key, and rapped out dots and dashes as though his hand had become electrified. However ordinary the message was, Bob treated it as if he were about to learn the secrets of the universe.

"Whatever comes across the wire, I'm the first fellow in Boston to know it," he said. "That's the reason why I love this job so much. Makes me feel spry."

I understood perfectly. The depot was an exciting place to work. Trains came and went all day, clanging their bells and shrieking their whistles, scattering cinders and smoke. And news of the trains came clattering over Bob's key. It was like seeing all the vastness of America come to life, and the telegraph was its voice.

A paper tape with the dots and dashes recorded on it came spooling off a reel whenever a message was sent or received, but no real operator looked at it. He knew what it said just by listening. Rattling out at over thirty words a minute at its fastest, the voice spoke of trains delayed or derailed, events and emergencies up and down the line.

Once, when Bob had stepped out for a few minutes and left me alone in his office, a message came over the wire that had to be answered immediately: TRAIN FROM NEW YORK DELAYED ONE HOUR STOP ADVISE STATION-MASTER STOP ACKNOWLEDGE IMMEDIATELY STOP

I went over to the key and tapped out, ACKNOWLEDGED STOP. Then I waited for Bob to come back. "Message came while you were out," I said. "It's on the tape."

Bob looked at the message and my answer. "Well, better tell the stationmaster." He went out again.

For a second, I had joined the voice. I had spoken to New York. I listened to a message for Hartford go clicking past, and felt mighty. I tried to explain it to Bob without gushing.

"Know how you feel," he said. "Fellow gets to miss it after a while. Time was, I used to work for the Baltimore & Ohio. They fired me. I went west lookin' for a job. One day, walkin' along beside the wires, I got so lonely for some news I cut into them and just listened for a bit."

"How did you do that without a set?"

"Put the ends of the wires on my tongue," Bob said.

"You're joking!" I shouted.

He bent over his key and disconnected it. Then he stuck out his tongue and placed the wires on it. "Train from Springfield's right on time," he said after a moment. He held out the ends to me.

I placed them gingerly against my tongue and felt a message from Albany coming in!

I kept thinking that one day I'd hear some news of John Brown over the wire. But Kansas was nearly quiet now. The Free-Soilers had won. The Congress had accepted their government at Lawrence as the legitimate one for the state, and the army had enforced peace. Most of the Border Ruffians had gone back to Missouri. So far, no state seemed ready to follow Kansas into bloodshed. I wondered what Brown would find to do now.

Then, one morning in early 1859, we had word of him. The whole country did.

My father opened his paper and exclaimed, "Well, I—" Brown was staring at him from the front page. A steel-cut engraving showed him with a long beard, looking very different now, wilder and fiercer. He did not seem like a man who would ever laugh, except, perhaps, at the death of an enemy.

At my mother's request, my father read the story aloud. Back in Kansas, Brown had started calling himself Shubel Morgan. He had recruited a few men and raided into Missouri around Christmas. He had attacked one plantation, killed the owner, and freed eleven slaves.

In the dead of winter, he had led his band north across the blizzard-driven plains toward freedom. They had hidden in freezing barns, traveling at night when they had to. Sometimes a farmer gave them a little charity. Finally, after eighty-two days and eleven hundred miles, he delivered the former slaves to the Canadian border. They had crossed that magical line and become free men and women in an instant. Not one person died on the way.

After giving the interview, Brown had disappeared into Canada himself.

My father studied Brown's picture closely. I saw his face tighten into the expression it had had the night Brown came up to us in the Congregational Church.

"I see Farmer Brown has undertaken to resemble Moses in looks if not in powers," he said. "No doubt his friends will be greatly impressed."

I put down my fork. "Who have you ever heard of who has freed eleven slaves?" I said.

"This business was not about freeing slaves," my father replied with a scowl. "It was about Mr. Howe and his crowd. Mark my words, Brown will be back in New England next, looking to raise more money for his next scheme."

"Brown is willing to risk his life for his beliefs," I said. "Next to that, money seems little enough."

"Money is no little thing, Theodore, as you will discover when you are responsible for making it," my father said. "And sending your son to school."

"Money is little enough when it is given for the right cause," I said.

My mother put her hand on my arm. In my head a voice cried, *You've never done anything in your life to free a single slave, Father. What right have you to sneer at those who have?* But I held my tongue.

"Excuse me," I said, and stood up.

"Sit back down," my father snapped.

"I prefer not to," I said, and headed out the door.

"Theodore, come back, please," my mother said.

"No," I said stiffly. "John Brown is a man I consider to be principled and heroic. I do not want to hear him insulted."

"Thee must not leave angry," she continued. "Thee and thy father must make peace."

I was too furious to answer. I grabbed up my books and headed for school.

The thought of it seemed more sickening than usual as I strode off down our hill. I was sure I'd finally throw an inkwell at Mr. Weems. I imagined doing that. I imagined what might happen to me if I did. Then the thought struck me—why go? Why not simply head for the Western of Boston depot and drop in on Bob?

It had never occurred to me to cut school before. Now

it seemed like an amazingly good idea. If I liked it, I might never go back. Why did I need Harvard if I had the telegraph? It struck me in that instant that I could simply walk away from my life with my key under my arm. I saw myself with a hat like Bob's, and a life as free as his. In an instant, I was whistling.

I heard Bob's voice in my head as I sauntered down the street. *Been on my own since I was twelve, and I'll be on my own till the day I die.... They always need operators. I can pick up and go whenever I feel like it. That's what you call freedom.*

I had the depot in sight when I saw two men walking toward me from that direction. I could not believe it. John Brown himself was coming up the hill, with Mr. Sanborn stuck to his side.

Brown's hand swooped up to his hat and waved it at me. Mr. Sanborn called out, "Young Master Worth," and ran to take my hand. "I was not aware you came this way to school."

"I have other business this morning," I told him.

"A very happy accident," Mr. Sanborn chirped. "You remember Mr. Morgan, of course?"

"Theodore, I am happy indeed to see you again," Brown said, grasping my hand and putting his other on my shoulder. "I want you to know, young man, that your five gold dollars were particularly well spent."

It was strange to meet him unexpectedly. The beard, although it did not hide his face, made him look like another man. The John Brown we had sheltered had looked dangerous but knowable. This man looked as though there was something inside that nobody knew.

But the deep voice was the same. The granite handshake was the same. I was glad to see him again, very glad.

Mr. Sanborn beamed at me. "Mr. Morgan told me that story. That is how I know you are a true friend."

"And how are all at home?" Brown asked.

"All fine, thanks," I said. I was hardly willing to say more. "I was very happy to hear that your—your adventure went so well."

"Oh, it was more than an adventure," Mr. Sanborn said. "He has proven himself all over again. I am telling you this only because I know you are one of the true ones." He looked around and dropped his voice. "But there are those here in Boston who were thinking of withdrawing their support. Important men. They thought Mr. Morgan was not reliable. That his plans were too extreme—beyond even his ability to carry out. Now they see differently. Now they know he can do whatever he sets out to do. First he must make another try at fund-raising. Then things will begin to happen. You will see."

"That's enough, Frank," Brown said, nodding his head in the direction he wanted to go.

"Yes. We must be leaving," Mr. Sanborn agreed. "There are those about who—well, you know Mr. Morgan's situation." He winked at me.

"I hope that we will meet again, Theodore," Brown said. "My best respects to your family."

He and Mr. Sanborn strode away through the crowd. I looked after them, before turning back toward the depot. If Mr. Sanborn had had a tail, it would have been wagging.

FIVE

Bob was surprised when I came into his office. "Why ain't you off in school learning something I can ask you about?" he said.

I told him of my words with my father. "I guess it must seem like pretty mild stuff to you," I said. "But I couldn't believe he said such small-minded things about Brown."

Bob shrugged. "Come on. If you're playing hooky, I reckon I can, too."

"You have your job," I said.

"Just watch the key for a minute," Bob said. He went out but was gone for much longer than a minute. A few messages came through, yet nothing that needed more than a short answer, which I could give. Soon something important would have to come over that key, though. I began to pace the crowded little room.

At last, the door opened, and Bob shoved back into the office with a tall, sleepy-looking man in his grasp.

"This is Wilson. He's coming in early to finish my shift. Ain't you, Wilson?"

Wilson didn't look all that happy to do it, but he sat

down at the key, put his hat over his eyes, and seemed to go back to sleep.

"Owes me a couple of favors," Bob said. "Glad to pay me back for one of them, aren't you, Wilson?"

Wilson shrugged and snored elaborately.

"Let's go, buddy," Bob said to me.

"Just like that?"

"Sure, just like that. You look like you need a friend today."

We hurried out of the depot into the bright spring sunshine.

We kicked down the streets that led to the harbor, stopping and looking at every common thing: huge coils of ships' cable, heavy wagons trundling along to the docks. It was all ordinary, and all new because we were doing it together and we were both free.

Eventually Bob took me to his room on the top floor of an old three-story house on a dingy street. It was dark inside and smelled stale, but Bob had paid for it himself and could leave it when he wanted. It seemed a noble place to me, in spite of the unmade bed with its thin mattress and the single oil lamp with its smoke-blackened chimney.

"What are we doing here?" I asked.

Bob grinned. "Getting a couple of things. I figured out a plan for today. Old Bob's going to expand your education." He pulled a spare railroad telegrapher's hat off a nail and put it on my head. I took the hat off and looked at it. The brass plate on the front said *Baltimore & Ohio R.R.*

"Looks good. Now we're both working," Bob said. He fetched a telegraph key from under the bed. It had a short roll of wire attached. "Come on. Remember when I learned you to read the wires on your tongue? This'll be better."

We headed back to the Western of Boston tracks.

"Now I'll show you something," Bob said.

He picked out a telegraph pole and climbed it like a monkey. He unlooped the wires of his telegraph key and twisted them onto the wire strung between the poles. Then he threw the key down to me.

It started to rattle in my hands.

"Pretty slick, eh?" Bob called down. "You can even send messages like this."

"What should I send?" I called back up.

"Nothing," Bob said. "It's something to know how to do, but only a dog'd send a bogus message."

"But then what's the point of showing me?" I asked.

"Well," said Bob. "Suppose you were somewhere else and you needed to get in touch with me. You could just hook up your key and get off a message, and sooner or later I'd get it."

I paid closer attention to the message coming through. It was just a jumble of numbers. It made no sense. "What kind of message is only a string of numbers?" I asked.

"Secret code," Bob said. "Some businessman doesn't want everybody else to know his business. Stockbroker, probably. Or banker."

Bob unwound the wires and shinnied down the pole. "Let's go," he said. We walked on up the tracks till we came to a pole that had a few metal spikes sticking out of it to make a ladder. "Up you go," Bob said.

"Me?" I said.

"I picked you an easy one. You ain't scared, are you?"

I was, but I couldn't let that stop me. I dragged myself up to the top of the pole and leaned heavily on the crossbar at the top. I wasn't very high, but I felt as though I were. I could see back the way we'd come to where the track curved, and up ahead all the way to the depot.

"Okay. Now do what I did," Bob shouted. I did, and threw the key down to him.

That's when I saw a handcar with four men aboard coming up the track. Two of the men, huge fellows, were wearing the uniform of the railroad yard police. When they saw us, they slowed down and stopped.

I thought, *Here's trouble.*

The policemen got off the car and came over to Bob. "What's going on?" the bigger one asked.

"Clarity test," Bob said. "Some of the signals are coming into the office muddy. We don't want that. Trying to trace down the place where the electricity's leaking."

The policeman nodded wisely, but his companion said, "Seen you before, but who's that?" and jerked his thumb up at me.

"Just helpin' me out. Used to work for the B. & O.," Bob said. "Might be able to use him around here. Hey, Jess," he called up, "this wire's all right. Come on down and we'll try up the line."

I detached the wires and hurried down the pole as fast as I could. The handcar went its way.

"That was top-notch lying," I said.

Bob shrugged modestly. "He's happy. We're happy. No harm done," he said. "Let's get something to eat."

It was long after noon, but I hadn't realized I was hungry until Bob mentioned lunch. "Well," I said, "I don't have much money today."

"I never do," Bob replied. "Come on."

Not far from the station there was a low, dark building with a sign in front that said CHEAP LUNCH. Bob plunked down a couple of nickels, and we fed ourselves at a long table piled high with the remains of platters of beef and ham and bread.

"This is a good place," Bob said. "One of my favorites."

I looked around. Food and sawdust covered the floor, and there were large damp stains of beer on the tables that were still cluttered with scratched white dishes and empty steins. We were almost the only people in the place, except for a couple of knots of men singing loudly and sadly in a language I didn't know. I fell in love with the place at once.

I wanted to do something to thank Bob. I felt in my pocket and found ten cents. "I'll get us beer," I said.

Ten cents bought a pitcher. I poured lavishly into the steins, jumping back when they overflowed.

"Okay, greenhorn, now let me show you something." Bob laughed. He refilled the glasses by pouring slowly down the sides. "See? This way you're not just getting the suds." He hefted his drink. "Here's how," he said.

I watched the way he drank and tried to copy it. Some of the foam went up my nose. I snorted and wiped my face with my sleeve.

"You'll catch on," Bob said. "It ain't real hard."

He was right.

When we'd finished the first pitcher, Bob got another. The day took on a glorious haze. I loved Bob. I loved the mysterious music in the corner. I loved John Brown, and Mr. Sanborn, and my schoolmates. I almost loved my father again.

"We need a secret code," I decided.

"What for?" Bob asked.

"In case," I said. "I mean, suppose one of us really needs the other."

"Kid stuff!" Bob snorted.

"It would be easy," I protested. "All we need is two *Webster's* dictionaries. I'll be Noah and you'll be Webster. That'll be the sign that what comes next is going to be in code. Every word is a three-number group: page number, column number, and number of the word down the column. Like this—" I tapped out, 25–1–6 STOP, on the table.

"And what's that supposed to be?" Bob asked.

"Page twenty-five, first column, sixth word," I said.

"Okay, okay," Bob said. "I ever get a message for Webster, I'll go right out and buy me a dictionary."

I went on tapping out Morse code on the table. BOB GIBBONS IS A GREAT GUY STOP.

Bob tapped back, THANKS ACKNOWLEDGED STOP AND I MEAN STOP.

But I didn't want to stop. I looked over at him as seriously as I could, and tapped, I SAW JOHN BROWN OUTSIDE YOUR STATION TODAY STOP.

SURE YOU DID STOP ARM IN ARM WITH PRESIDENT BUCHANAN STOP, Bob tapped back.

"No, really," I said. "It was him sure as I'm sitting here."

"Some guy who looked like him," Bob said.

"I know John Brown," I said. "He stayed with my family once. That's a secret, though."

"Tell me another," Bob said. "Your old man hates Brown—you told me so yourself. So what would he be doing in your house?"

I told him the story.

"Well," Bob said, shaking his head, "guess if I gave room to somebody like Brown, I'd keep it a secret, too. Man ought to be hanged."

"What?" I was sure I'd heard him wrong.

"Stole eleven slaves according to the papers," Bob said. "Killed their owner. You should have turned him in when you saw him."

"For freeing slaves?" I said.

"Owning slaves was still legal last I heard," Bob remarked. "If he'd stolen eleven horses, what would you call him?"

"But Bob—human beings aren't horses."

Bob laughed. "Hell, I saw slaves all the time in Baltimore. Didn't look so bad off to me. They sure weren't running off to Canada."

"These slaves thought differently," I said.

"How do you know? If a crazy old white man comes riding onto your place with a gang, shoots your owner, waves a gun at you, and tells you to come along, you'd do it, wouldn't you?"

"You—" I stuttered as though I'd made a great discovery, "you're not an abolitionist, are you?"

"Hell, no," Bob replied. "We've always had slaves in this country. Always will have. Hell, Boston needs a few slaves. Folks'd calm down about it if they saw what they're talking about."

"We had slaves in Boston once. We freed them. That's because we saw slavery was wrong. That's why there are abolitionists. That's why I am one."

"Slavery wrong? You never even asked most people what they thought," Bob shouted. "It was just a few of you swells that decided for everybody. Ask a workin' man what he thinks about slavery. Like those guys in the corner. Or those cops we talked to today. Or me. Most people don't give a damn for abolition, even in Boston. And those that do don't know what they're talking about. Like you." Bob was glowering at me.

"And what do you know about it?" I asked, glowering myself. "You saw slaves, but did you ever talk to any? Or ask them how they felt? And if they're so damned happy, why does it need a federal law to bring them back if they run away?"

"I didn't say they were happy. I said they weren't so bad off," Bob said. "Slavery suits 'em."

"Bob, you're the freest man I've ever met," I said. "Can't you see that other people want their freedom as much as you want yours?"

"Then why ain't they got it?"

"Because—because they'd be killed if they tried to take it," I said.

"There you go. They'd rather be alive than free. And that's what they are."

"But in your heart—" I began.

"I've got a white man's heart."

What I did next was unforgivable. Drunken. I tossed my beer in Bob's face.

He sat there for a second, looking stupid with surprise. Then he uncoiled his right arm and hit me square on the eye. The blow knocked me backwards.

By the time I got to my feet, Bob was already on his.

"You want to go 'round, I'm ready," he said, his fists clenched and cocked. His eyes were red hot.

If I'd been sober, I'd have tried to apologize. But I

wasn't sober, and I was furious. "To hell with you," I said.

The singers had stopped. They were standing up now, watching us and grinning.

"Finish him off," one shouted.

"Give it to him," another said.

"Go on, get out of here," Bob muttered. "And don't come back when you're sober. Damn abolitionist."

I made my way to the door, hardly seeing. A wave of ugly laughter pushed me out onto the street. The light hurt my eyes.

With my head spinning and anger choking me, I staggered off. There was nowhere to go but home, and I couldn't go there. Not as I was. I needed to sober up and to think of a good lie to tell. Bob would have had one at the tip of his tongue. "Clarity test. Some of the signals are coming into the office muddy." I shook my head and it spun. My eye hurt.

Beer, despair, and anger overwhelmed me, and I bent my head over the gutter to retch. I told myself I felt better afterwards, but I didn't.

SIX

By late afternoon, I had thought of a lie. I had stayed late at school to work on my geometry. My eye was black from a badly thrown ball. I squared my shoulders and marched into the house.

I stopped as soon as I opened the door. Mother was standing in the parlor with Amy and Talitha clinging to her dress. My father had his arms around her. They were all in tears.

"Where have you been, you rascal?" my father roared. He stalked across the room to me.

"At school—" I began.

"I see very well what kind of school you have attended today," my father said. He swept his arm in front of me, and Bob's spare hat flew from my head and bounced against the wall. Somehow, it had stayed on my head all day, until I had forgotten about it. He stared me in the eye and smelled my breath. "Drinking, fighting. A fine education. Exactly what I feared would come of your 'hobby.' And you've brought home a trophy to commemorate your achievements. Tell me, did some low friend give you that hat, or did you steal it? Never mind, this is no time—"

My mother pushed past him, fell on my shoulder, and sobbed, "Theodore, thy grandfather Evans is dead. We have just had the telegram."

I had hardly known my mother's father. He and my grandmother had moved to Cincinnati when I was very small. I had only vague memories of a short, lively man with a sharp nose. Yet I felt as though something had been ripped away from me.

"Your mother and I must discuss the mourning, Theodore. Mind your sisters."

He took my mother into another room while I sat down with Talitha and Amy. They had not met their grandfather Evans, but they had never seen their mother so anguished. They were crying from fear. Nothing I could do would comfort them. They kept trying to jump down from the sofa and follow our parents. Every time I brought them back, they screamed more loudly.

At last, Mary came in to rescue me, with milk and a gingersnap for each of them. When she saw my eye, she brought a piece of beef for that. The girls calmed down enough to eat, and a little later, our parents came back.

"We have discussed what is best to do," my father said. "Your mother must go to Cincinnati for a time to be with her mother. We cannot all go; tickets for that would be too expensive. Therefore, I will stay here and look after the girls. Theodore, you will go with your mother to support her. You will leave as soon as we can find a train going west."

"There's a night train to Albany on the Western of Boston," I said. "It leaves at 9:10."

"Indeed," my father observed. "You are amazingly informative on some subjects, Theodore. One wishes you were as well versed academically. Well, that leaves us very little time. Go and pack one bag. Don't take your good suit; you'll be measured for mourning in Cincinnati."

"Surely I could leave tomorrow morning, Hale," Mother protested. "There is so much to do here."

"You will have to rely on me to see to it, Caroline," my father said, taking both her hands. "Your mother needs you most now. And I will do the best I can."

"Yes, Hale."

Mother went upstairs to pack.

I went to my room with one of our old carpetbags and stuffed it with nearly all the clothes I owned. By the time I was finished, the bag was bulging and I could barely close it.

My mother came downstairs in her black mourning dress. She would wear black for a year from this night.

"Put this on, Theodore," she said, handing me a black armband. "It will serve until thee have thy new suit."

We ate hurriedly. In the middle of the meal, Mary came back into the dining room.

"Beg pardon, but there's a young man to see Master Theodore. He says he'll wait," she said.

It had to be Bob.

My father gave me a hard look. "We will interrupt our meal, Mary. Come with me, Theodore."

Bob stood up when we came into the room. " 'Scuse me, Mr. Worth. I'm Bob Gibbons," he said. "Ted was down at my office earlier and left these." He held up my schoolbooks.

"It was good of you to return them, sir," my father replied coldly. "He will be spending more time with them in the future than he has in the past. He also has something I believe may be yours. Fetch the hat, Theodore."

When I brought it, Bob took it and said, "Thanks. It's mine. Ted, about today, I—"

"Then I believe our business is concluded," my father interjected. "My son is breaking off his connection with you. We are not accustomed in this house to drunkenness, fighting, and lying. I trust it will not be necessary to meet in the future, sir. Good night."

With a sigh, Bob turned and went out. My father looked silently at me for a long time. "This is disgusting and shameful," he said at last. "Have you forgotten who we are? Or do you simply not care anymore?" He held up his hand to cut off my answer. "I have nothing more to say on this subject. We will not mention it again. It goes without saying that you will stop your telegraphical nonsense at once and spend your afternoons henceforth in preparing for Harvard. Now we will go back in to your mother. Try to be a comfort to her, at least."

I sat at the table in misery for a few more minutes. Then a wagon came and took us to the depot. As we jolted away from home, my mother began to cry again.

The depot at night was the same scene of passengers and freight that I had seen scores of times, but somehow it was different now. Details I had not noticed for months stood out boldly under the gaslights.

I was full of sorrow and shame, but I could not help feeling a little excited. I had never left Boston before except to visit Concord or Cambridge across the river. Now in less than two days I would be in Cincinnati.

My mother bought our tickets. They were twenty dollars apiece. No wonder only two of us were going. Even in good times a hundred dollars for such a purpose would have been something to think over. A well-bound novel from our bookstore cost two dollars at the most.

There was little to see as we pulled away from the depot. Only the Charles River stood out, a wide swath of absolute darkness between the dim lights of Boston and the towns across from it.

My mother sat looking straight ahead. At last she said, "I wish so much, Theodore, that thee had known thy grandfather better. I often thought to take thee to visit, but I kept putting it off. I wanted more money in the house, or a more convenient time. Now that there is almost no money, and no time left at all, we go. I have been a fool."

It struck me that my grandfather, who had been a prosperous man, could have come to visit us, but I didn't say so. I simply put my arm around my mother's trembling shoulders.

There were sleeping cars on the train, but we did not pay the extra cost of one. We would spend the night sitting on hard red velvet seats, getting what rest we could. The train jerked and rattled, the engine rumbled and hissed, and the clack of the rails marked time for it all. It was more loud and uncomfortable than I had ever imagined, but we were making a steady twenty-five miles an hour. Tomorrow morning would find us in Albany.

My mother slept at last, but I couldn't. I felt betrayed by Bob, but I missed him. I was angry with my father. I was ashamed of myself. I felt the last of my drunkenness slowly leave my head, and as it lifted, felt the weight of my grandfather's death come down more heavily.

We reached Cincinnati late in the afternoon. At the train, we were met by a staid, middle-aged black man in top hat and frock coat. He had a mourning band like mine on his sleeve.

Tipping his hat to my mother, he said, "Have I the honor of addressing Mrs. Worth and son?"

My mother nodded.

"I am Jacob, ma'am, an employee of your mother's. Please come with me."

Jacob carried my mother's luggage to a fine-looking coach in front of the depot. The horses' harness was draped in black. The coachman was much younger and lighter-skinned than Jacob, but I saw a strong resemblance.

Jacob climbed up beside him, and we started off.

The streets of Cincinnati were crowded with people and wagons of every kind. On all sides, I saw fine new red brick buildings and the steeples of churches. There was a sense of bustle about the city that made me like it at once. Its people seemed to have come from everywhere. I could hear the accents of New England and the South on the streets. And repeatedly I heard German. The signs on the stores were in German almost as often as English.

Then I saw something that stood out even here. A gigantic birdcage of a building with a sort of minaret, the tallest thing on the street. I craned my head back to look at it again and wondered what it could be.

My grandparents' house was an immense place, with a deep porch running all along its front and sides. Perhaps it circled the building—I couldn't tell. There was a similar porch for the second story. The roofline was broken by a squarish six-sided tower. From this, and along the roof, ran a narrow widow's walk with an iron railing.

The house was generously supplied with chimneys, tall windows, and elaborate wooden scrollwork. It would have looked much like a Mississippi riverboat, except that the windows had all been shuttered for mourning. I was impressed, yet I wondered what kind of Quaker my grandfather had been. It wasn't the Friends' way, or Boston's way, either, to spend so much money on show.

But the outside of the house was nothing compared to the splendor beyond the entranceway. Even the vestibule was paneled in some rich, dark wood. The double doors that led into the rest of the house were a deep rose. The parlor to which Jacob showed us was as heavily furnished as a palace. There were so many sofas, tables, thick stuffed chairs, and fire screens that it was almost impossible to turn around.

"Mother, I never realized Grandfather was so rich," I whispered.

"We never were before," my mother said. "Nothing like this. It does not feel like home. I cannot see a single thing that I recognize."

There were two large portraits hanging over the fireplace. One was of a smiling, white-haired woman with her hand on a dog's head. The other showed a dapper little man leaning easily on a bale of cotton. My grandparents.

My mother went to the fireplace and looked up at the painting of her father. "Dearest one," she said, "please forgive me that I did not come before now."

Behind us Jacob said, "Mrs. Evans, ma'am."

I turned. My grandmother looked much like her portrait, but she was bent and unsmiling now. The same dog, old and bony, shuffled into the room after her.

She and my mother clung together.

"I thank God that thee have arrived safely."

"We had a good trip. Mother, this is thy grandson."

My grandmother took my hand and studied me. "A good face," she said at last. "Mostly Worth, but there is Evans enough in it. Thee are a very welcome sight, my boy."

"Thank you, Grandmother," I said, and kissed her lightly on the cheek.

Something pushed against my leg. It was the dog's nose. He wagged his tail slowly.

"Tiger likes thee. That speaks well of thee. He likes only gentle people."

She sat heavily on a chair so tall she almost disappeared into it. "The funeral is tomorrow," she said. "We hear the will afterwards. I have seen it. Thee will be well pleased, I think."

My mother started to cry once more.

Quietly my grandmother told us about my grandfather's death. He had been down on the landing, helping a gang unload cotton bales, when his heart had failed him. "It was a place he loved to visit," Grandmother said. "And the men thought it a good joke that one of the richest men in Cincinnati would play at longshoreman with them. But he was very strong for his size."

I glanced up to see Jacob nod.

After a while, Grandmother said, "Shall we go in to see thy father?"

I couldn't avoid it, of course. This was why we had come.

Jacob helped Grandmother out of her chair and led us into the back parlor. There was a coffin in the middle of the room, set on a catafalque draped in black. The coffin was also solid, shining black, with silver handles. Black candles burned at its head and foot.

I had never seen a dead body. My grandfather looked very small lying on the satin lining. His long nose was bigger than ever in his shrunken face, his skin covered with chalk. He did not really look like a man anymore. It was like looking at a huge, grotesque doll.

We sat on small, hard chairs. Grandmother and my mother were, I supposed, waiting for the inner light to inspire them with something to say. I was conscious only of the heavy heat and the silence in the parlor.

After what seemed to be a long time, Jacob put his hand on my shoulder and whispered for me to follow him. He led me up the stairs to my room, which, with the gas turned all the way up, was brightly lit. I could see through the cracks in the shutters that the sun was setting.

There were three men waiting for me there. Two had tape measures and bolts of black cloth. The third had a large pile of shoes.

"These gentlemen are here to provide you with mourning, Master Worth," Jacob said. "Because the funeral is tomorrow, I took the liberty of making the arrangements myself. These are Mr. Zimmermann and his assistant. The gentleman with the shoes is Mr. Schaeffer."

In a few minutes, Mr. Schaeffer had tried on several different pairs of fine black shoes and found one that fit me beautifully. They had high tops that ran up past my ankles.

Next, the tailors took my measurements and marked up some of the cloth with chalk. They went out of the room. In a few minutes, I heard the whir of a sewing machine down the hall.

"Mr. Zimmermann and his assistant will, I believe, require an hour or so to prepare your suit," Jacob said. "Until then, I will return you to the corpse."

But I didn't want to go back into that hot, still parlor just yet. My curiosity was bursting. "Jacob," I said, "could you tell me something about my grandfather? I hardly knew him."

"I shall try, Master Worth," Jacob said. "What is it that you would like to know?"

I blurted out, "How did he get so rich?"

"Hard work, Master Worth," Jacob answered.

"But in what? What did he do for his money?" I asked.

"Chiefly, he speculated in cotton, I believe," Jacob said. "Cotton and wheat. But chiefly cotton. He also exported luxury goods to the plantations. Iron lawn ornaments and the like."

I remembered the portrait of Grandfather leaning on a cotton bale. No wonder he'd built a house that looked like a riverboat. The wealth that had made him had flowed up from the slave states across the river. I saw it suddenly—this house was built on the labor and blood of slaves.

Quakers were abolitionists. But Grandfather had apparently seen nothing wrong in making a fortune based on slavery. I felt sick.

"But, Jacob—you are free, aren't you?"

"I am, Master Worth," he said calmly. "Is there anything else you would like to know? I am sure your mother and Mrs. Evans will be grateful for your return."

I let him lead me back through the darkened house to the parlor where my grandfather lay.

I don't know how long we sat there. I tried to feel sorrow, but I kept thinking of how my grandfather had made his money. How had he justified it to himself? Had he ever been bothered by what he was doing? If so, when had he changed? His coffin was silent, full of secrets. I was very grateful when Grandmother finally announced it was time for bed.

Jacob woke me early. I got up, feeling I hadn't slept at all. The morning was quiet but hectic. The undertakers came to set out a huge feast in the dining room, and people arrived to pay their last respects and to visit and eat. The tailors came back to make a few alterations to my suit.

I went downstairs and was introduced to dozens of white-whiskered gentlemen who shook my hand and called me a manly chap and told me what a fine man my grandfather had been. At last it was time for the funeral procession.

This was the biggest parade I had ever seen, bar the Fourth of July. Grandfather led off in the hearse with high glass sides, plumes, and black bunting. Four matched black horses drew it. Professional mourners in tall black hats trimmed with crepe marched along behind. A line of carriages came next, with the three of us in the lead. There might have been fifty others, all decked out in black.

The procession looped through the downtown and back again. We interrupted traffic for blocks. Many men stopped to doff their hats as we passed. I felt foolish and exposed sitting in our open carriage. My mother's eyes were dim, and she was hunched over, facing me. Grandmother's veil was so heavy, I couldn't see her face.

At last we returned home. I had thought that we were going to one of Cincinnati's new cemeteries, but I was wrong. Grandfather had had a tomb built for himself and Grandmother on a little hill behind the house.

Twelve pallbearers carried the coffin to a catafalque set up at the door to the tomb. The building was of polished granite with a couple of columns flanking a shining bronze door, and so tall it seemed top-heavy. On the lintel above the door was the word EVANS carved into the stone and gleaming like gold. Below, in smaller letters, ran DEUT. 23:15–16.

Standing waiting for us at the door was a tall, fat man in some sort of clerical clothing. He conducted an elaborate burial service that no Quaker would have approved of, in a heavy Southern accent. It was full of high-flown language and came out of a book. In the middle of it, he preached a long sermon on the holiness of my grandfather's life. What anyone else thought about it, I couldn't tell. My own thought was that, somewhere in his life, Grandfather had ceased to be a Quaker.

At last, it was over. My grandmother thanked "The Reverend Mr. Barnes" for his kindness in preaching, even though Grandfather "had not been of his flock." Barnes smiled and simpered and assured her that it had been his privilege and honor.

Everyone left, and we went back to the house to hear the will read.

The lawyer was a little man with immense muttonchop whiskers and no other hair. He had pale, bony hands with rings on most of his fingers.

"I am happy to be able to inform you that the late Mr. Evans left you all exceedingly well provided for," he said. "It is indeed fortunate that there are so few among whom to divide his generous estate."

He rustled his papers and began: "'I, William Evans, being of sound mind and body, do hereby bequeath all my worldly goods to my dear wife and companion, Elizabeth Evans, with the following exceptions. To my loving daughter, Caroline, I leave the sum of ten thousand dollars in gold—'"

Mother gasped. Then she began to cry again.

The lawyer went on, "'And to her son, my much missed Theodore, I leave my best watch and the sum of three thousand dollars in gold, to be paid to him on the day of his graduation from college or at the age of twenty-five, whichever shall come first. I leave as well any small personal item my wife may think fit to give him.

"'To my dear granddaughters, Amy and Talitha, I leave the sums of three thousand dollars in gold each as dowries to be paid on the occasions of their marriages. Finally, to my son-in-law, Hale Worth, I leave my best thanks for the care he has taken of my daughter and the fine children he has brought into the world.

"'I regret now that, in my enthusiasm for my business, I never returned to Boston to renew my connections with you, but God is calling me back to a home that is even older than Boston. Farewell, my dears.

"'Your affectionate husband, father, and grandfather, William Evans.'"

The lawyer left, and we all sat with our thoughts. I had never imagined so much money. And so much of it for me. It didn't seem quite real. I wished I had known him. I wished he had come to visit us.

But perhaps it wouldn't have mattered. I would have been a child, with a child's vision. I would have loved him more but not known him any better. No, I was never going to know what kind of man William Evans, Friend, businessman, and profiter in slavery, had been really. Had he been a hypocrite, or had he simply not been able to see his connection to a thing he knew was wicked? Or had money answered every question for him?

At last my grandmother spoke: "Well. It has grown late. I suggest we all go to bed. Tomorrow will be better. Let us make it come a little sooner."

I did try to sleep. I lay on top of the covers for hours, pretending to ignore the heat and the stale air. I held absolutely still, telling myself I didn't notice the sweat running off me. The air grew worse.

Finally, I drifted into a doze. But on the edge of sleep, I heard the house creak in some far corner. I jerked awake, thinking of ghosts.

There was no point in trying to sleep now, I decided. I got up and raised the window in my room. I pushed open the shutters. No one would know if I mourned my grandfather with the window open.

It was balmy for March, and I held out my arms to the breeze coming up from the river. The moon was half-full but so bright that I could see every detail in the yard below.

I don't know how long I leaned on the windowsill, but

shortly before the moon went down, I saw three figures run across the lawn and disappear behind the house.

A shiver of fear went through me. A moment later, I heard Tiger bark. It was a tired noise, the sound of a dog who didn't really care who was in his yard. Nothing else happened as far as I could tell.

I didn't know what to do. I couldn't wake Mother and Grandmother and frighten them with what I'd seen. Nor did I want to admit I'd opened my window. Jacob and his son seemed to be the only men around the place, but where were they? I didn't even know where they slept.

I lit my candle, pulled on my pants and shirt, and slipped into the hall and down the stairs. The thick carpets muffled my steps. The heavy front door unlocked quietly, and I edged through it, blowing my candle out.

Now I felt well and truly scared. There was no sign of anything in the front yard. I crept around the side of the house where the three figures had gone. There was nothing to be seen there, either. Only a few trees and my grandfather's tomb.

I waited for a while in the shadow of the house, but nothing moved in that quiet place. I decided to go back inside. Then from the tomb I heard a cry.

I froze. There was no mistake that the sound came from behind the brass door, so faintly that in daylight I would never have noticed it. It came again.

Why I didn't run I do not know. Probably I was too frightened. But the third cry, louder than the first two, made me realize what had happened. My grandfather must be trying to get out. He had awakened in his coffin and was trapped in his own monument. Such things happened. I had to rescue him.

I ran to the tomb. The bronze door had a huge leverlike handle so big I needed both hands to move it. But it moved. I heaved on the door and pushed it slowly in.

"Grandfather?" I said. "Grandfather?"

Seven pairs of eyes looked back at me. No faces, only eyes. The cry came again. It was not a man's voice. I took a step back and bumped into the door frame. Then a dim red light glowed in that awful place, and I saw a face I knew.

"Go back to bed, Master Worth," said Jacob. "There is nothing here. You have seen nothing. Go to bed."

Behind him, a baby whimpered. Half a dozen dim shapes were holding their breaths.

"Jacob, my grandfather—" I began.

"Is in Heaven with the just," Jacob said. "But those he has left behind must do his work. Your part is to go to bed. Now." He gently pushed me out the door and closed it behind us. "Allow me to escort you back to the house."

As we rounded the front of the house, Jacob looked up at my open window. "So. Master Worth, I believe your grandmother would be very distressed to know that you had neglected your mourning. I suggest that neither of us say anything of these events to her. Do I have your word as a gentleman?"

"Yes," I said. "Only, what is going on?"

"Good night, Master Worth," Jacob said, and left me.

SEVEN

 I slept little that night. There must be some way, I thought, to warn Grandmother that her faithful servant was up to something behind her back. I had to find it.

When I came down to breakfast, Jacob was standing by my grandmother's chair.

"Thy mother and I have sad work to do this day, Theodore." She surprised me by smiling. "We must go through thy grandfather's things. There is no need for thee to be here. I shall have Jacob's son Joshua show thee Cincinnati."

"Respectfully, ma'am, that will be difficult for Joshua," Jacob said. "He has much work to do with the horses. I should be very glad to escort Master Theodore."

Grandmother nodded slowly. "Very well, Jacob, if thee think best."

When breakfast was over, he and I set off on foot. Our steps took us down broad streets lined with mansions into the center of town.

I felt sure that Jacob was anxious to keep me under his eye. And, since I knew he wouldn't answer any questions about what I had seen last night, I wasn't going to give him the satisfaction of asking them.

I was struck again by how busy Cincinnati was and how quickly it appeared to be growing. The city was not much older than I was. The fine stone houses I saw, decorated in the German style, and the college, churches, and theaters, had not been here when I was born.

Jacob didn't mind how long I took to examine the sights we passed. In fact, he took me out of our way to show me some of them. And he answered any question I asked him about what I saw. But all his answers were carefully considered, and as formal as if they came out of books: "This building, Master Worth, is a *verein* hall. German workmen build them as places to meet and to study. There are several in Cincinnati, each built by men of a different trade. . . . This spot, Master Worth, is where the original fortifications of the town were set up. It was a log palisade with loopholes for guns. I do not believe that it was ever attacked." After a morning of this, it struck me that Jacob would have been a great asset to Mr. Weems.

But even Jacob's pedantry couldn't kill my interest. The finest thing of all, when we reached it at last, was the river. It was a powerful dark gray, with the green hills of Kentucky rising on the far side. There were steamboats everywhere, coming and going and tied up to the wharves in front of us. They filled the sky with their smoke and called to each other with their bells and whistles. They were smaller and rounder than the Mississippi riverboats I had heard about, but they looked grand enough to me.

There were warehouses and stores all along the waterfront, full of goods and buyers. About half of them seemed to have the word *Kanawha* in their names.

I tried it aloud: "Kanawha."

"If I may, Master Worth, we pronounce it Kanawha," Jacob said. "It is a river that flows into the Ohio some miles southeast of here in western Virginia. It is a region united to us by trade."

I looked toward the river, where a gang of black stevedores was unloading cotton from one of the riverboats. They were chanting a work song, only a few words repeated over and over. I wondered, *Are they slave or free?* I glanced at Jacob but could not read his expression.

Somewhere on that noisy wharf, another song started. Low, throbbing, and full of yearning. I had never heard anything like the sorrow in it.

> *Deep river,*
> *My home is over Jordan,*
> *Deep river, Lord,*
> *I want to cross over into campground,*
> *I want to cross over into campground.*

For a moment, the whole waterfront seemed to stop and listen. Then a steam whistle rose over the words and those who had listened turned back to their work.

It was late afternoon now, and Jacob suggested that we should go back to Grandmother's. But there was one more thing I wanted to see first. Something I had noticed on my first day in Cincinnati.

Even in a town full of ambitious buildings, this one stood out. It was three stories tall and crowned with a dome like something from the *Arabian Nights*. There was a deep granite porch in front. It sat on its lot at the corner of Third Street like a toy a giant had put down and forgotten. I wanted to know what it was.

When we reached it, I saw that the doors were heavily locked. Shrieks and wails came from inside. The word ASYLUM was painted over the door.

"What is this place, Jacob?"

"It is a madhouse, Master Worth."

"But why would anybody build a madhouse that looked like this?"

"It was not one originally," Jacob said. "It was, in fact, a museum. Your grandfather told me that an English female writer, a Mrs. Trollope, built it. Have you heard of her?"

I had heard of Fanny Trollope and of her son, Anthony, the novelist. But to come upon this connection with them here was astonishing.

"A museum? What kind of a museum?" I asked.

"She tried various things to attract the local people," Jacob replied. "The one that worked best was the Last Judgment. There were large paintings on glass of Heaven and Hell, and live actors moving among them. There was even a devil with an electrical pitchfork. I have been told that people came back time and again to see it."

To go from a museum of damnation to a madhouse seemed logical somehow, but frightening. It was as if the power of Hell had been tempted to this spot and been made real.

I noticed for the first time that everyone crossed the street to avoid this place.

"Let's go, Jacob," I said.

"Very well, Master Worth."

Three men who had been lounging in the shadows across the street caught up to us as we started toward home. One was a little gray man who barely came up to my shoulder and was bone thin. The other two were much bigger. One had a scraggly black beard, the other pale eyes and oily blond hair.

"Where you goin', boy?" asked the little man in an accent I had never heard before.

"I beg your pardon, sir?" I said.

"This nigger yours?" the little man said.

"We are both free men," I said. "Good-bye."

The three of them laughed.

"Both free, eh?" said the little man. "Well, I reckon we'll take your word—about you."

Suddenly Jacob broke into a run. Before he had got ten yards, the black-bearded man had hold of him and the third man had lifted him off the ground with his arms twisted behind his back.

"Let him go!" I shouted. "Help, murder!"

" 'Tain't murder," the little man said, grinning. " 'Tis returning property to its rightful owner. We're slave catchers, you see."

"But Jacob is free, I tell you. He works for my grandparents."

People were stopping to watch, but no one crossed the street to help. The two big men began hustling Jacob back toward the river.

"This man is being kidnapped," I called. "Someone help us, please."

No one moved. A few laughed.

"See, boy, those folks know the law better than you do," rasped the little man. "It's a mighty serious thing to interfere with a officer of the law in the process of his rightful duty. You could go to prison for it, by the laws of these here United States. But seein' it's your first offense—"

The pain shot up my groin and I bent double, letting out a sad little gasp. Then I felt a knee in my face. A blow pushed me into the dirt.

"Hold on just a minute," cried a big wagoneer with a whip in his hand.

Thank God, I thought, and tried to stand up.

"What proof you-all got?" said the wagoneer.

"All we need," said the blackbeard. But they stopped.

"What proof?" The wagoneer shook his whip.

"Got a paper here for a runaway slave just his height an' age," said the little man. "Want to see it?"

"Can't read," said the wagoneer. "But it don't matter. Probably ten hundred men in Cincinnati like him."

"This is the one we want," said the little man.

The wagoneer turned to me. I could almost stand straight again. "You say he's free?"

"Yes, damn it," I coughed out.

"Let's see his back."

The little man slit Jacob's clothes up the back with his Bowie knife. Jacob's skin was trenched and welted by whips. The scars were old.

"Fancy work," said the wagoneer. "Well, if he ain't your runaway, he's somebody's." He gave me a dirty look. "Lyin's a great sin, boy. For all your fancy clothes, you're less than a man like me. Don't forget it."

The three slave catchers hauled Jacob to the river while I struggled behind, calling for help. A few bystanders looked on; others turned away. No one took a step toward us.

There was a dirty little sailboat tied up at the wharf. The blackbeard leapt aboard and snatched up some chains. Jacob was bound wrists, feet, and neck. He had said nothing all this time. But when the chains were locked onto him, he threw back his head and howled.

"You'll pay for this," I shouted. "I'll rescue you, Jacob. We'll get lawyers—"

The little gray man said, "He's snug now, Burl. You can belt that boy if you want. Don't cripple him none, though."

The big blond climbed back onto the wharf and in one motion lifted me off my feet. I swung at him, and he laughed. Then he sat down on a barrel, turned me over his knee, and pulled down my pants. His hand was like iron.

After he'd had his fun, he threw me to the ground and kicked me.

"Jest you lay there till we're gone," he said. "I see you get up, I'll whup you good." He jumped back into the boat.

I stood up as they pushed off. "I'll have you for this," I shouted. "I'll have you all for it."

Jacob looked back at me, despair in his face.

The slave catchers laughed, and then they were beyond hearing me. I watched as they edged out into the strong current some yards offshore. I saw the little boat swing around, and the men turn their attention to the rudder and sail. That was what Jacob was waiting for. As soon as they took their eyes off him, he jumped.

He made one great splash and disappeared. He'd never had a chance, and he knew it.

The little boat crossed to Kentucky.

EIGHT

It was dusk by the time I limped back to the house. As I came up the street, Joshua was cantering toward me on the bare back of one of Grandfather's horses.

He pulled up when he saw me. "Master Worth, you are hurt," he exclaimed, sounding just as Jacob would have. Then, "Where is my father, Master Worth?"

I leaned against a picket fence for support and dropped my eyes. "Jacob's—*dead*. He ... we ... slave catchers near the river ... I tried ..."

Joshua whipped his head from side to side like a hunted thing.

I reached up for his hand and clutched it. "I tried. I tried, but ..."

"No," Joshua said, his eyes glistening with tears. "You're wrong. You must tell me so, Master Worth. Please."

"I'm sorry," I said. "I tried. There were too many for us."

"Slave catchers? Slave catchers killed my father?"

Joshua was on the ground beside me now, hanging on to me.

"No," I said. "He killed himself."

"He would never do that," Joshua shouted.

"They tore the shirt from his back. They saw his scars," I said. "No one would help. When they put chains on him, he jumped in the river."

Joshua collapsed against the side of the horse and wept, pounding his fists into the animal's side. The horse bent its head around and nickered at him. It pushed its nose against his face.

I did not know what to do. At last, I put my arm around Joshua's shoulders.

The door to the house opened.

"Theodore?" my mother called. "Theodore, what is wrong?"

"Joshua," I said to him. "Joshua, we have to tell the others."

Without Jacob, the whole household seemed to collapse. The dignified mourning for my grandfather evaporated. All of the silent and almost invisible servants suddenly appeared and wandered up and down the halls weeping. I cried more for Jacob than I had for my own grandfather. They were tears of rage at the slave catchers, the wagoneer, and at the people who'd stood by and watched. I hated Cincinnati now. I hated my country, where what had happened to Jacob was legal. The slave catcher had been within his rights.

The next day, Grandmother called all the servants into the front parlor. She gave them train tickets to Canada and money to get started there. "There is no safety here anymore for thee," she told them. "There never was. And without Jacob and my husband, there is no keeping their work going. I am too old and too weak in cunning, and Joshua cannot do it alone. Go and find thy true freedom."

There was more crying then, and a great deal was said that I did not understand. Joshua swore that he would never leave. "They can't stop us, ma'am, and you can't make me go. We can keep the work going. Don't send me away."

My grandmother only shook her head.

People began to leave the house later in the day. I felt the life seeping out of the place. Early that night, Grandmother called Mother and me into the parlor in the back. She had a few things stacked on a little table beside her chair.

"I would have thee know about my husband," she said. "Thee have seen how we live. It is not exactly according to how thee were brought up, Caroline. Thee may think that thy father had forgotten who he was. He had not." She stopped, cried a little, and then went on. "Thy father and Jacob were stationmasters on the Under Ground Rail Road. In our years here in Cincinnati, they saved more than one hundred poor souls out of bondage. They used his fine tomb to hide them."

I understood suddenly. Grandmother would have known well enough what old Tiger barked at that night.

"Thee have seen the verses cut over the door of his tomb," she went on. "They were his little joke. Here, read them." She took a Bible from the table and handed it to us.

15 Thou shalt not deliver unto his master the ser-
vant which is escaped from his master unto thee:
16 He shall dwell with thee, even among you; in

that place where he shall choose in one of thy gates;
where it liketh him best. Thou shalt not oppress him.

My grandfather had rescued more slaves than old John Brown. He had borne the disdain of other good men and pretended friendship with bad ones, all to save men and women from bondage.

Mother's eyes were shining. "Mother, I thank thee ten thousand times for this," she said. "Thee has given me my old, true father back. He was a better man than I ever knew."

"He was the best man," my grandmother said. "But his work is ended now." She put the Bible back and handed me a leather tube with brass fittings. "This is for thee, Theodore. I am sure thy grandfather would want thee to have it."

I opened the tube and slid out the finest spyglass I had ever seen. No Boston ship's captain could have had a better one. It telescoped out nearly the length of my arm, and when I put it to my eye, the flocking in the wallpaper stood up like wheat.

"It's wonderful, Grandmother," I said. "Thank you."

"I hope thee may find a use for it."

Grandmother quickly hired some white servants to replace the others. But things did not go as smoothly as before. The new help had everything to learn. Mother took over their training, and so we had to stay in Cincinnati longer than she had planned.

I tried to make myself useful, but there was little for me to do. My best help seemed to be to stay out of the way.

I took to sitting with Tiger in the garden or on the steps of the tomb. I brought along books from Grandfather's library, but I didn't finish any of them. I brooded for hours on what had happened and on what I could have done differently. I wondered what I would do now. Only one thing seemed clear to me. If I had had old John Brown's pistol with me that day, Jacob would still be alive.

Brown was the man I should talk to, I decided. He would understand. He could advise me what to do. When we got back to Boston, I would track him down, no matter where he was.

We returned home. My days there were slow and very much alike. The last weeks of school crawled along. A glorious spring went by outside my window, but I barely noticed. I spent my afternoons studying, since there was nothing else to do with them. My telegraph key was locked up in a closet in my parents' bedroom, and Bob was out of my life.

My father announced that he was well pleased with me. I didn't care. After Cincinnati, nothing in my old life seemed to matter. It was too small for me now.

I wrote to everyone I knew who might know where Brown was, asking for his address. Those who answered wrote only to say they did not know. I was sure they were lying, but there was nothing I could do about that. Brown might as well have been on one of the stars I looked at through my telescope at night.

Then Julia Ward Howe came to call on my mother. Normally, I had nothing to do with visits from my mother's friends. This time, I found excuses to stay within earshot of the parlor. Mother's version of our trip to Cincinnati left out a great deal. She said nothing of Jacob's death or of the Under Ground Rail Road. Mrs. Howe was all sympathy and courtesy, and stayed exactly the proper length of time.

As she was getting ready to leave, I appeared at the door and said, "May I walk you home, Mrs. Howe?"

My mother smiled. Mrs. Howe thanked me.

When the door closed behind us, I said, "Mrs. Howe, I would like to tell you some more things that happened in Cincinnati. My mother did not mention them, perhaps because she did not see them, but I did. And because I saw them, I need your help, if you will give it. I want you to intercede with your husband for me."

"Whatever can you mean, Theodore?" Mrs. Howe asked.

"I saw a man die rather than be taken back into slavery," I said.

"Dear God!" she gasped. I waited. "And what do you want Dr. Howe to do?" she said finally.

"Only to give me John Brown's address. He has refused to do it already, but perhaps if I could tell him the story, he would relent."

Julia Howe shook her head. "I do not follow you. Why should you need Mr. Brown's address?"

"I want his advice on how to proceed," I said.

Julia Howe looked at me quizzically. "Proceed with what?"

"I want to know my best course as an abolitionist," I said. "I think he is the man to tell me."

Julia Howe regarded me gravely. "Mr. Brown leads a dangerous life. People who are near him may be in danger, too. As you already know."

"You and your husband don't mind it," I said.

"We accept it," Mrs. Howe said. "But the rest of your family does not see things as we do."

"I do not see things as my family does," I replied.

"I am torn, Theodore," she said. "When we reach home, come in. Tell your story to my husband. I think he must decide whether to help you."

I waited while Mrs. Howe found her husband. When at last Dr. Howe appeared, he sauntered into the room, his wife following. He was prepared to be polite to an excitable boy.

"So, Theodore, I understand from my wife that you have had a most terrible encounter in Cincinnati," he said. He made a little temple of his fingers and bent forward. "I should very much like to hear it from your own lips."

"When I was in Cincinnati, I met a man who worked for my grandfather. A free Negro named Jacob," I said. "A quiet man. He seemed unfriendly. The night of my grandfather's funeral, I heard noises outside the house and went to see what the matter was. I found nothing outside, but I heard a wail from my grandfather's tomb. I found the door unlocked, and some people inside. Jacob was with them. He would tell me nothing, but escorted me back to the house and made me promise to say nothing of what I had seen. The next day, he took me walking in the town. Down by the waterfront, slave catchers attacked us. I told them Jacob was free, but they ripped the shirt from his back and discovered whip marks. That was all they needed. They took him aboard their boat and chained him. Then, when they turned their backs for a moment, he jumped into the river and drowned. I had to carry the news home to my grandmother. She immediately dismissed all her servants and sent them to Canada. Then she told us that Jacob and my grandfather had been stationmasters on the Under Ground Rail Road."

Chev Howe's back was straight; his fists were clenched and his eyes burning. Mrs. Howe moved over to the little sofa where I sat and took my hands in hers.

"If I had been there, boy, there would have been blood," Howe snapped.

"Since that day I have been thinking what would have happened if John Brown had been there," I said.

"Ah, Brown. Now there would have been the man to have at your side," he said.

"Dr. Howe, I need to find John Brown," I said. "I have to find my own way to fight slavery. And I think John Brown is the man to tell me."

Dr. Howe did not answer for a long time. Then he said, "Brown is not an easy man to find. And he is at present very busy on work that I will not discuss without his leave to do so. Indeed, I do not know much about it," he said with emphasis. "But knowing what little I do, and knowing your father, I think I must regretfully decline to help you."

"Dr. Howe, I am not my father," I said.

"You are quite right, Theodore," he said blandly. "But you are not quite yet your own man, either."

"Good night, then," I said, getting up and heading for the door.

"If there is any other help or advice I can give you, please come to see me again," Dr. Howe said to my back.

Mrs. Howe came to the door with me. "What you have seen makes me want to do anything I can to help you," she whispered. "But I fear what may come of it if I do."

My heart leapt. "There can be no danger to us in a letter or two," I said.

"There isn't, if it stops with that," she agreed. "If I help you, you must promise me it will go no further than letters. I value your trust, Theodore. Please, for your mother's sake, do not betray mine."

I said nothing. Mrs. Howe bit her lip.

"He stops sometimes at a hotel in Springfield," she said, and gave me its name. "Remember to address your letter to Shubel Morgan."

NINE

To my surprise, I heard from John Brown within the week. His letter lay on the tray by the door, with the rest of the morning mail. The paper seemed to glow in my hand.

North Elba, N.Y.
June 15, 1859

My Dear Young Friend,

I have just received yr. letter and will be most happy to see you again. It fills my heart to think of those events in Cincinnati, and I understand how it is that now you wish to do something against such men. I am home at present on business which I cannot confide here. If you can come to my farm at North Elba, we may talk about it. Come soon if you can, as I do not expect to be here much longer.

Your Friend,
John Brown

P.S. Bring your telegraph. J.B.

I needed to be alone to think. I went out the front door and jumped down the steps into the street. I walked around the block three times before I was calm enough to look at the letter again. Then my brain started to work.

If I was going to make my way to upstate New York, I needed to start soon, and I needed money to get there. My parents would look for me, of course. I must do something to throw them off my trail, and I must travel fast. After a long time, I had worked out a plan. I went back into the house.

Mother was sitting in the front parlor, sewing a dress for Talitha. The bright fabric spilled across the floor in the sunlight. She made a happy picture sitting there, but her face was drawn and pale.

"Thee have had a letter from John Brown," she said.

"How did you know?" I asked.

"Julia Howe told me what name he is using now."

"I wrote to him on a private matter," I said.

"I fear to ask what that matter is, Theodore." She studied my face for a long time. Then she said, "Theodore, do not thee remember thy grandfather? Did he not save more poor souls out of bondage without violence than John Brown has with it?"

"I think that only John Brown has an answer for the men who killed Jacob," I said.

My mother closed her eyes and bent her head to her hand. "That answer is death," she said.

"If John Brown had been with me and Jacob that day, no one would have died," I said. "Those slave catchers would not have dared to attack us. Jacob would be with

Grandmother, helping more people to freedom and taking care of her."

"It is a hard thing to reject violence in a good cause," my mother said quietly. "But violence is never just, Theodore, even in the best cause. And it rarely achieves anything but more violence. Mr. Brown is a brave man and a good one, but it was votes, not bullets, that made Kansas a free state."

"It was Brown's guns that protected the voters," I said.

"Have thee prayed for thy inner light?" Mother asked.

"Yes," I lied.

"I hope thee are telling me the truth, Theodore," she said. "But I fear Jacob's death has killed something in thee, too. Dearest one, do nothing from hate."

"I promise," I said, lying again, "if you will promise not to tell Father about this letter."

"I cannot do that," Mother replied. "Thee should talk with him about this."

"No," I said. "He hates Brown."

"He does not hate Brown," Mother said. "He fears what Brown would do if he had the power."

"If Brown had the power, he would free all the slaves," I replied. "Doesn't Father want that? Don't you?"

Mother looked away and shook her head sadly. "It is not like me to keep secrets from thy father. And I am not sure thee are telling me the truth. But I will promise to keep this secret." She sighed heavily.

I kissed her cheek and went out of the room. I had to work quickly.

Money was the first and easiest of my problems to solve. I took Grandfather's beautiful telescope, extended it one last time to its full length, closed it, and slid it into its tube. Then I went down to the waterfront and sold it to a clipper's first mate for ten dollars. Together with the two dollars I had saved, it should be enough.

Now all I needed was my telegraph key.

There seemed to be no way to get it. It was sitting in a locked closet, and I rather suspected my parents wouldn't open that particular closet for me. I wandered around Boston Common, trying to think of how it might be done, and came up with nothing.

Then two words from the past came back to me. "Clarity test," I whispered. One well-told lie could solve my problem.

The next day, about two in the afternoon, I ran into my father's office.

He was busy with his red and blue pencils and some author's manuscript. He looked up and raised his eyebrows at my interruption.

"Father, Mother has misplaced her keys and sent me to borrow yours," I blurted out.

"That is very unlike your mother, Theodore," he said. Still, he reached into his pocket.

"I'm sure they'll turn up," I said. "I'll bring these back shortly."

Father nodded and resumed his work.

It was a hot, heavy afternoon, and Mother and the girls were sitting under the trees behind our house. It was the easiest thing in the world to go upstairs and unlock that closet door. My telegraph key was there, as I had known it would be. It felt good to hold it again. I tapped it twice and smiled.

I returned to my father. "Here," I said, handing him the keys, "and thank you."

"And where was your mother's set?" Father asked.

"They fell out of her pocket when she was hanging out clothes," I said.

He shrugged, and I left, to seek the best way to North Elba.

There were seven railroads leading out of Boston, but not one of them went near the place. It lay at the edge of the Adirondack wilderness. The best way there was by stagecoach to Lake Placid, about three miles beyond it. From there, I would have to walk back. I paid for my ticket on the next day's early coach.

June twentieth dawned hot. I was up before then to leave a note on the kitchen table.

> *Am gone West to try my luck. Don't worry—I have my key.*
>
> *T.*

Talitha's and Amy's voices followed me downstairs. "Where are you going, Theodore? Why are you up so early? We want to come, too."

"I'll be back soon," I called, reflecting briefly that lying was becoming rather easy for me, with relatively little practice. Perhaps I had a talent for it.

The night before, I had hidden my bag, with my key and some clothes, under a bush in the yard. I snatched it up now and made my way swiftly in the direction of the stage station.

The coach was leaving just as I ran up. The driver

threw my bag on top, and I jumped in. I was the only passenger.

The driver started with a jolt that threw me hard onto the seat, and we were off, bouncing over the cobblestones so that my teeth rattled.

It took three days to reach Lake Placid, and by that time I was heartily sick of stagecoaches. To ride in one was to spend all day being shaken like a rat by a terrier, except that this terrier could shake up to a dozen unfortunate passenger-rats at once, all knocking into each other. By the time we reached Lake Placid, I was as glad to see the place as if I were returning to a much-loved home.

I walked back to North Elba, a small village of five farms on poor soil. I found a room in a house for the night and counted the hours until morning.

While I was waiting, I practiced with my key, getting the rust out of my fingers. It felt good to be tapping out the Morse again. Once or twice a wave of regret rose up in me at what I had done, not so much to my parents as to my sisters. I thought of their bewilderment and fear and longed to go back home and take them in my arms. But these times passed, and I stayed where I was.

The next day, I made my way to John Brown.

A long road ran straight uphill toward the farm. It stood alone at the foot of a mountain, not a high one, but steep. Any marshal or sheriff coming near would be visible a long way off. The farmhouse was low and unpainted, with a chimney at either end and a scraggle of trees behind it. There was nothing unusual about it except for a huge rock leaning against one side.

I knocked. A girl opened the door. She had black hair and froglike eyes. "Good day, sir," she said.

"My name is Theodore Worth," I told her. "Is Mr. Morgan in?"

"You may call me Brown up here," said a voice from the back. John Brown came and stood in the doorway. "Come in, Worth." He smiled. "I expected I'd see you here."

The inside of the house was almost as barren as the mountain. It was dark and drafty, and full of people.

A man with a shotgun and hard eyes came over and shook my hand. "Jeremiah Anderson," he said. "Pleased to know you."

I was sure he had been holding that gun on me as I came up to the door.

Brown introduced me all around. Besides Anderson, there was Brown's handsome son Oliver, who sat close by his new wife, Martha. They were as fine-looking a couple as I have ever seen. The girl who had answered the door was John Brown's daughter Annie. She was a little younger than I, and followed her father adoringly with her huge eyes. Her sister Ellen, next in the circle, looked about four. Their mother, Mary, nodded silently to me. She had a fine, strong face and had cut her hair very short. Last, there was Owen Brown, his shoulders bent, his hands nervous.

As for Brown himself, he looked different again. I noticed for the first time that he was not as big as I had remembered. I recalled him as nearly a giant, but he was almost exactly my height, and I am not tall. His beard was short now and grayer. He was aging. But when he took my hand, I felt the power in the man. Nothing had touched it. I thought he seemed fiercer than ever.

We all followed Brown into the kitchen, like filings after a magnet, and Annie made some tea. Brown told everyone a couple of stories from the time he'd spent with us. He seemed to remember every detail.

"You will eat with us and spend the night," he said to me. "Tomorrow, we will have time for some private talk."

I was given a place at the table next to Brown. When our plain meal was finished, everyone gathered around the fire. The family treated Brown like visiting royalty, I thought. Annie waited on him hand and foot, though she seemed to be everywhere else at once, washing dishes and cleaning up. Oliver stayed close to his wife, but kept his eyes on his father and never made a move without his say-so. Mary Brown sat by her husband and worked on a pile of clothes needing to be mended, talking about things on the farm, but speaking only when Brown spoke to her.

Brown spent most of the time after supper paying attention to Ellen. He took her on his knee and played and sang to her in his strong, flat voice. He was as tender and gentle as a man can be with a child, but Ellen seemed a touch frightened, as though she had seen so little of her father that she didn't really know who he was. Finally, he asked her, "Would you like your old father to lift you up on his hands?"

Ellen gravely shook her head no.

"My dearest little one, you need never be afraid when I am with you. I once lifted Mr. Worth's two little sisters up, one on each hand. Isn't that so, Worth?"

"Yes," I agreed, and added, "they still talk of it."

"Come, I will show you how I do it," Brown said, and lifted Ellen almost up to the ceiling. He set her gently down, and she immediately ran to her mother and hid her face in Mrs. Brown's skirt.

Anderson and I sat together. He stationed himself closest to the door and kept his shotgun by him. I had seen no dog on the farm, but perhaps with Jeremiah Anderson they didn't need one.

"Were you in the fighting in Kansas?" I said, trying to start a conversation.

"Oh, yeah," he said.

"Was it bad?"

"It's always bad," Anderson said.

After that he withdrew into himself and was silent until he announced he was turning in.

"I should, too," I said.

"Wait," said Annie, and lit the stub of a candle for me. It was in an old pewter holder with the handle broken off. "I reckon you'll bunk with Mr. Anderson. Good night."

Our bed was just big enough for the two of us. I blew out the candle and lay down with my back to Anderson. I felt very strange to be sleeping next to a man who hadn't exchanged more than a sentence with me all night.

"Good night," I said.

"Night," Anderson agreed. Then he added, "Don't worry about the fighting. You either do it or you run. Real simple."

I soon heard his breathing change to the long-drawn rhythm of sleep. Then I slept, too.

Breakfast came early and was quickly over. When we were finished, Brown said, "Come with me, Worth. I'll show you a bit of the farm."

The wind was blowing so hard we almost had to shout over it. Even on this sunny morning, the air felt cold. Small clouds came and went swiftly.

"I am sorry about your grandfather," Brown said as we took in the view down the road to North Elba. "I never knew mine, but he was a hero to me. Was and is. He was a captain in the Revolution." He put a hand on my shoulder. "Does your family know where you are?"

"No," I replied. "They think I've gone West with my telegraph key."

"Well," said Brown, "they aren't fools. They will be looking for you here pretty quickly, I expect. No matter. I shan't be here."

"I am sorry to have caused you any trouble," I said.

Brown laughed. "Half this country wants to kill me, and the other half wants to turn me over to those who do," he said. "I reckon you are not much more trouble."

"But that's not true," I said. "You have support all over the North."

"I can always draw a crowd," Brown said. "I suppose that is a kind of support. But it is not what's needed. What did Chev Howe tell you?"

"Only that you were busy at something he didn't know much about."

Brown's body rocked with one of his silent laughs. "That's Chev," he said. "Well, he's right. He knows little enough. And the less he knows, the happier we both are."

"But doesn't he give you money for your work?" I asked.

"Oh, yes. Some. And Sanborn and a few others. But they don't necessarily want to know what I do with it," Brown said. "And I am not inclined to think that they should. It makes some folks nervous to know too much."

Brown shrugged and swung his arms irritably. His face looked grimmer than usual for a moment, and he went on. "I was almost set to go South in '57, but the business panic dried up my money. And a fellow I'd hired to train my volunteers went to my supporters—Chev Howe and Frank Sanborn and the others—and told them that if he didn't get more pay, he was going to run down to Washington City and squeal like a stuck pig. When they wouldn't pay, he went to Senator Sumner and told him all about it."

"And then what happened?" I asked.

"Well," Brown said, "they are all fine gentlemen and are a little worried about being associated with anything that might land them in prison. First, they cut back on the money they'd already promised me. Then they told me that they would have nothing to do with such plans, if they knew about them. So we agreed that, in the future, they would not know about my plans."

"My father thinks you mean to split the Union over slavery," I said. "Is that what you hope to do?"

"I think this country is split apart by slavery already," Brown answered. "And the slave owners know it. Look at the army. Every department but New England is commanded by a Southerner. The Southern secretary of the army is transferring weapons into Southern arsenals. The

Southern secretary of the navy has sent all our ships into far waters. The Southern secretary of the treasury is draining all our money into Southern banks. They know what they are doing. So should we all."

He fixed me with his hunter's eye. "Some of us would split this country to keep slavery alive. Others would risk splitting it in order to kill it. What would you do?"

"Anything I could," I replied. "I hate all slaveholders."

"Careful, youngster," he said. "Don't let hate get a grip on you. Anger yes, but not hate. I never yet killed a man because I hated him."

This answer, so much like my mother's warning, stunned me. "But didn't you hate the men you killed out in Kansas?"

"No," Brown said. He leaned closer to me. "Now, let me tell you a story. My boy Frederick was killed about a year after Osawatomie Creek. Shot on his own front porch one morning by some Missourians. They were taking revenge. We knew who had organized it. We tracked that man to his farm, and one of my men put him in the sights of his rifle. But at that moment I forbade the killing. He did not own slaves. I saw that to murder him would not have advanced our cause. So I let him live. Hew to the one task, Theodore, and you will never go far wrong."

"But what task is that?" I asked. "That's what I need you to advise me on. How can I best serve the cause of freedom?"

"That all depends," Brown said slowly. "Are you a Quaker like your mother?"

"No," I said.

"Then can you kill?"

That stopped me. "I don't know," I said at last.

"That is a thing to know," Brown said. "Do you remember the day I put the pistol in your hand years back?"

"Yes," I replied.

"If you had had it in Cincinnati, would you have used it?"

"Yes," I said. I felt sure of that.

"Then you have the answer to my question," Brown said. "Come along." And he led me in the direction of the barn.

"For twenty years or more I have had a plan," he continued. "I have studied it and researched it. I have visited the fortresses of Europe and read all the books I could find on guerrilla warfare. Do you know what kind of warfare that is?"

"No," I admitted. I didn't know then that there *were* different kinds of warfare.

"It is the war of the weak against the strong," John Brown said. "The war of the ambush and the quick, small raid. It is the kind of war my grandfather fought against the redcoats. We won one war for freedom with guerrilla tactics. We can win another."

"What is your plan?" I asked.

"That is as much as I can tell even a friend," Brown said. "It is better not to know too much of it at once. Besides, plans must change sometimes to fit circumstances. But I will tell you this: I think I have the right to require a few men to be as dedicated as myself to the work, so long as I ask nothing of them that I would not do.

"This fight runs in my family," Brown went on, unlocking the barn door. "Do you know much about the Alton Riots?"

"A little," I said. "Men in Illinois killed a minister for printing an antislavery newspaper. That was in '36, I think."

"Thirty-seven," Brown said. "I was living in Ohio then. My father and I were in church when the news reached us there. I stood up, raised my hand, and said, 'Here before God in the presence of these witnesses, I consecrate my life to the destruction of slavery.' Then my father got up. He had a terrible stammer and didn't love to speak in public, but he said, 'When John the Baptist was killed, his disciples took his body and laid it in the tomb and went and told Jesus. Let us go to Jesus now and tell Him,' and the congregation sang mightily as we went up to the altar, my father and I, and knelt there. That is the kind of men I need, men who have knelt at that altar."

"Captain Brown," I said, "will you take me along when you start your war?"

He cocked his head at me. "Captain? Yes, Worth, you may call me captain now."

In the light from the open door, I could see stacks of long wooden cases. The lid on one case was loose. Brown lifted it up and handed me what was inside.

"Sharps rifle," he said. "Most accurate weapon in the world. Loads from the breech, so it fires five times as fast as a muzzle loader. Here, look at these."

From another case he took out a long pole with a Bowie knife blade attached. He tapped his finger against the blade, and it rang. "Bell metal," he said. "The finest. I have these and five hundred more coming."

I took it from him. "But Captain, are pikes useful in war nowadays?" I said.

"They are as I will use them," Brown said. "For a

brave man who does not know how to shoot, a pike may serve well until he learns. Militia, you see, won't stand up to bayonets. A thousand free men charging with these can scatter their enemies like dust."

The wind keened through the barn, whistling and sobbing.

"This is what it must come to," Brown said. "This is what it must be. Can you do it?"

I thought a long thought. It was a desperate thing, but not impossible. There must be more to this than I could see. More men, somewhere. More weapons to come. Under this man, who had already done so much, we could finish the job. We could shake slavery apart. I was sure of it.

"I will kneel at the same altar," I said.

Brown nodded. "We will leave tomorrow morning."

We started back to the house. We stopped by the immense rock that leaned against it. The name JOHN BROWN was cut deep into its side. I felt something go cold inside me.

"That was my grandfather," Brown said. "Captain John Brown, who served Connecticut in the Revolution. About a year ago, I had the stone moved here and my son Frederick's name carved on the back of it. When I am dead, this stone shall cover all of us." He patted it.

There was a grim smile on his face. A cloud passed overhead, and for an instant Brown and the stone were the same black mass. Then the sun came back.

"It will be a fine thing to lie here when all is done," Brown said.

PART TWO

The Invisibles

TEN

Two rivers came together, making a point of land as sharp as a spear. Along both banks of the point the arsenal buildings were strung out, in neat red brick. The town filled in the space behind them and ran up the hill beyond. It was as pretty a spot as any in America.

"What rivers are those?" I asked.

"The big one is the Potomac; the smaller one is the Shenandoah," Brown answered.

This was my first look at the valley, though we had been nearby for two weeks now. Brown had spent nearly every day scouting with one or two of the others, but I had been kept at the farm he had rented eight miles away in Maryland. Sometimes I had been the only one there, and I hadn't liked being left behind. But today I was part of the deception.

"How well is the arsenal guarded?" I asked.

"A few night watchmen is all," said big, blond John Cook. "I've made friends with a couple of 'em. Nice old fellows. I would hate for 'em to get hurt."

I had met Cook just that day. He had been living in

Harper's Ferry for a year, spying for Brown. He was an outgoing man, and everyone in town liked him. He had even married one of the town girls.

"None shall be hurt, I hope," Brown assured him. "We want no battle here."

Looking down into the valley below us, I could see why. Its sides were as steep as a bowl's. Only three ways led out of it by land, and only two of those were any good. The third, which we were on, was a rugged track that led into the mountains. It would be easy to be trapped in a place like that. I was glad Brown was an expert raider who always left himself a line of retreat.

"And there are no regular troops in the area closer than Washington City," John Kagi said happily. He was Brown's second-in-command. He had joined us last night at the farm.

"Regulars," Brown snorted. "A few dozen marines, you mean. Guarding ships' stores is all their soldiering. And no militia anywhere. Not that I give spit for militia."

"Still, when the day comes, we must be quick," said Kagi, stroking his fine brown beard. "Once we seize the arsenal, we must begin work at once to get away. We won't be safe until we're up in these mountains behind us."

"Oh, there'll be time enough to get out," Brown said. "There's no one to stop us."

"Still, we must be quick," Kagi said.

Jeremiah Anderson started to unpack the extra horse we had brought. He handed me a rock hammer, while Brown, Kagi, and he set up surveying equipment.

"I thought we were cattle buyers and farmers," I said.

"So we are." Kagi grinned. "But we also drop hints

that we are prospectors. It gives folks a reason why we are out and about scouting so much. And the rumors that we're looking for gold cheer everyone up."

"I like to make folks cheerful," John Cook said.

The sound of horses coming up the road caused us to turn. There were six riders, all carrying pistols and shotguns. Chains clanked at their saddlebows.

"Morning," said their leader, reining up beside Brown.

"Good morning to you," Brown said.

"Seen anything of two niggers go this way?"

"You are the first people we have seen this morning," Brown answered.

The man looked hard at us. "You ain't from around here," he said.

"I rent a farm a few miles north," Brown said.

"The old Kennedy place?"

Brown nodded.

"I heard of you," the man said. "Well, if you didn't spot 'em on the road, check your barn and henhouse when you get home. There's money in it if you catch 'em. Fifty dollars apiece."

"Indeed," said Brown. "And how would we know them?"

The man handed over a poster with two descriptions on it: *CUJO, about twenty-five, medium height and build. Very thick arms. CASSIE, about eighteen, light complexioned, about five feet. If taken, contact the sheriff or Mr. Hiram Harris, Waverly Plantation. $50 reward each.*

"And you gentlemen have hopes of catching them?" Brown asked.

"Oh, I guess we will," the leader said. "We run down five last season, didn't we, boys?"

The boys all nodded, and one let out a long, drawn-out whoop.

"I was not aware that slaves had a season," Brown said.

"Well, you'd better know it if you're goin' to live around here, mister," the leader said. "Fall's the time the owners sell their extra slaves south. Some of 'em don't take to the idea of goin' to Mississippi, and run off. Mostly, though, what happens is one of a pair gets sold and the other one hangs itself. That's what the season is."

"We thank you for the information," Brown said. "If we run into these two ungrateful runaways, we will certainly know how to treat them."

The leader stuck out his hand. "Brannan's the name, Captain Bill Brannan," he said.

Brown took it. "I am Isaac Smith."

"Remember what I told you, Smith," said Brannan. "Fifty dollars apiece, if we don't catch 'em first. Come on, boys." They rode off north.

"I thought you said there were no militia here," I said.

"Slave patrollers. Less than militia," Kagi replied.

Brown was wiping his hand on his pants. "Scum of the South," he said. "Scum of the earth."

Brown and Kagi passed a telescope back and forth, arguing quietly about which route to take into town, where to post guards, and other things. I eased myself off my horse for a short rest. I wasn't used to riding yet.

The arsenal turned out as many as ten thousand rifles a year and stored them there. That made it important in our plans. It was reassuring to know that Brown needed tens of thousands of weapons. I could not see how we were supposed to transport them up this muddy ditch and into our mountain fortresses, but I was certain that Brown knew. Soon, soon, I told myself, men like Captain Brannan would be running for their miserable lives.

That July day was the last time I was outside in daylight and good weather for three months. When we got back to the farm that afternoon, Brown said to me, "You will have to stay in the attic now, except at meals. There will soon be too many of us to come and go as we please."

The thought of being confined in that place seemed almost like being buried alive. I spent nights there already, and that was not bad, but never to leave it, except to go downstairs? "But what about Kagi and Cook?" I protested. "What about Owen and Anderson?"

"Kagi's going back to Pennsylvania tonight," Brown said. "As for Cook, you know he lives in town. I and a few others must be able to move about and spread false stories of what we're doing here. But you and those who are coming must hide. If the local people get a hint of what we're up to, they'll burn us out."

So I nodded and climbed the stairs to the long, dark attic.

Anderson and Owen spent their nights there, but I was alone much of the time at first. I saw the others at breakfast, where Brown led the prayers and the discussion. Then they would go off on their scouting trips, and I would be left alone with a drill manual and a Sharps rifle for company until night. When Brown didn't want Anderson with him, he and I would drill together. Anderson taught me how to use the Sharps, as well as he could in an attic. Sighting at a shiny penny nailed to the far wall, I would click the trigger and tear through the motions of opening the breech, sliding in a cartridge, and sticking on a new percussion cap. I learned to fieldstrip my rifle and clean it. Soon, I was an experienced Sharps-shooter in everything but the one thing that counted.

I was running through the manual of arms one day when a new man climbed into the attic. He was a gaunt-looking mulatto well into middle age. He had a thin bedroll on his back and one of our Sharpses.

"Dangerfield Newby," he said. "The captain sent me up."

I put down my rifle and stuck out my hand. "Thank God for some company," I replied.

Newby's face creased into a smile, and we shook hands. He put down his bedding next to mine.

"Captain Brown said you'd show me how to handle this," he said, lifting his rifle.

"As much as I know about it," I replied, and as quickly as that I was converted from recruit to veteran.

No one ever had a better pupil. Newby watched every move I made and copied me perfectly the first time. His concentration was amazing.

"You've done this before, I would guess," I said. "You're very good."

"I have to be," was all he replied.

That night, Owen and Anderson came back, and I introduced them.

"Know anything about when we start fighting?" Newby asked us.

We shook our heads.

"Can't be too long, can it?"

"I suppose not," I replied.

"You from around here?" he asked.

"No, from Massachusetts," I said.

"Ohio, mostly," said Owen Brown.

Anderson shrugged. "Indiana for a start."

"So far away," Newby mused, as though we had said "Mars." Then he took each of us by the hand, taking ours in both of his. "Thank you," he said.

"For what, Mr. Newby?" I asked.

"For coming down here." He picked up his rifle again and stroked it. "I'm free," he went on. "My father freed me when I grew up. But my wife's a slave, so my children are slaves. Their master means to sell them into Louisiana. He'd sell them to me if I had the money. That's a joke. Where am I going to get money for a woman and seven kids? So I'm joining up with the captain. If we win, I get my family back. That's my reason to be here. But you others came down to free all the families."

Owen, Anderson, and I couldn't think of anything to say to that, so we all just sat together in the dark, feeling each other's nearness. But that moment was the one that founded Captain Brown's new company.

Other men came in ones and twos in the next weeks and crowded into the attic. We were a strange collection: tough veterans of the Kansas wars, farmers, poets, and a former slave. There were the Thompson brothers, Bill and Dauphin; Charlie Tidd, Francis Jackson, Barclay and Edwin Coppoc. Another of Brown's sons, Watson, came, and we knew that John Jr. would be joining us before we went into action. There was Albert Hazlett, who had fought under Brown before. An odd bird named Stewart Taylor was a Canadian and a spiritualist.

These men were white, but blacks came, too. Besides

Dangerfield Newby, there was Shields Green, who had worked for Frederick Douglass, and handsome Lewis Leary and his brother-in-law John Copeland, both from Ohio.

We drilled every day. Brown's old military adviser, the one who had gone bearing tales to Senator Sumner, had written the manual we used. When Brown was there, he barked out the commands. When he was away, we took turns giving the orders. "Right shoulder arms! Left shoulder arms! Port arms! Order arms! Right about-turn! Left about-turn!" for hours at a time.

At first I couldn't see the use of so much of this kind of training. In the cramped attic, we couldn't even march. But as we trained together, the spirit that had begun the night Newby came grew stronger, and the drill helped build it.

We were very different men. We argued with each other about everything, and we even teased each other, but always as friends. I had never had so many friends before. I stopped being lonely, and at times was as happy as I'd ever been in my life.

Until the day Bill Leeman came.

I was lying on my blankets studying the drill manual again. Leeman thrust his narrow face up through the floor, sniffed, shrugged, and coiled the rest of his long, thin body into the attic. Then he glared down at me and put his hands on his hips. He had a whip looped through his belt, and a magnificent beard that looked brand new.

"What are you doing here?" he demanded in a strong Maine accent.

"What?" I said. "Studying the manual. Would you like to see it?"

He took it, scowled at the page I'd been reading, and said, "Book soldiering. I didn't need this in Kansas, and I sure as hell don't need it now."

"We're all supposed to learn it," I said. "Captain's orders."

"Don't tell me about the captain," Leeman said with a sneer. "I've rode under him." He threw the book back at me. "See this whip? I made it. I'm a whip maker. Just stay out of my way, boy."

"That's going to be difficult in the circumstances," I said. My voice was steady, but I was shaking. Why was he attacking me?

"Just see you do it, boy," he said, and turned his back on me. "Hey, Hazlett," he said. "Haven't seen you since Lawrence."

From then on, Bill Leeman insulted me at every chance. If I made a mistake at drill, he was sure to smirk and make some crack about "the boy." And he liked to stare at me and stroke his whip.

Although I could tell that the other men didn't like what Leeman was doing, it was clearly up to me to stop him. But how? I didn't understand where his anger was coming from. If he'd been a fat, cowardly bully out of a book, it would have been easy to know what to do. But Leeman was as lean as a snake and really had been a hero in Kansas. I couldn't help thinking that something in his warrior's eye told him I was no good.

I tried to think of what Bob would have done. One thing I was sure of, he would never have stood it. He would have put Leeman in his place with a few smart, tough insults or pitched into him with his barroom fighting skills. But neither of those were talents of mine.

I wasn't the only one Leeman seemed to hate. He hacked on Dauph Thompson and Barclay Coppoc, until Edwin stood up for his younger brother. He ragged on Stewart Taylor, too, but then almost everyone did that.

We couldn't help teasing Taylor. He was such a pompous little fellow that he may not even have realized we were doing it. Perhaps that's why he never seemed to mind. And pompous or not, he was one of us. In fact, in a way, he was the one who gave us our name.

We were dipping our rifle barrels in a mixture Cook had learned about at the arsenal. The stuff turned them brown, which minimized glare when aiming. Taylor wiped off his barrel, slid it back into the stock, and announced, "Men, I have been thinking."

"Thought we'd made you promise to stop that," someone drawled.

"Our company needs a name," Taylor went on. "A name as glorious as our cause. What do you say to 'The Liberty Grenadiers'?"

"I say *haw* to 'em," Bill Leeman replied. "That's as mush-mouth a name as I ever heard."

"There's a militia company back home calls itself the Invincibles," Dauph Thompson offered.

"Invincibles?" I said. "Hidden up like this, we ought to call ourselves the Invisibles."

We all laughed except Taylor. "You lack seriousness of purpose," he told us, but from that time on, we called ourselves Captain Brown's Invisibles.

The question was whether we could stay invisible as our numbers grew. Some of the local people began to suspect there was more happening at the farm than Farmer Smith was letting on. One old woman was especially troublesome. She was a toothless, ancient-looking crone with a company of greedy children. Hardly a day went by that they didn't come by to poke around and ask to "borrow" things.

Brown couldn't both keep watch on the place and come and go as he needed. Besides, with the attic full of men, the house was in chaos. So Brown sent for Annie.

The day she came, she bounced into the attic, looked around, sniffed, and declared, "You men had better give me your bedding and clothes quick. And don't hold anything back if you know what's good for you."

We did as we were told. We knew what was good for us. She was. Annie became our housekeeper, cook, laundress, and watchdog. Very often in the middle of one of our drills, Annie's head would suddenly thrust up through the trapdoor and hush us. We would all jump for our bedrolls and lie there, barely breathing, with our rifles held tightly along our legs while she dealt with the old woman.

Later, Oliver's wife, Martha, joined us and Annie had some help. It seems ridiculous now, but all John Brown's great plans depended on the courage and brains of two girls in their teens. We Invisibles relied on them for everything, from our breakfasts to our lives. In all the weeks we hid there, we never missed a meal, and we were never discovered. If there were any invincibles on that farm, they were Annie and Martha Brown.

That stinking attic was becoming hard to bear. There was no privacy at all. We breathed each other's air. The days dragged by, and our sense of danger grew.

Leeman became more and more morose. "I don't like

being cooped up like this" became his constant complaint. "I'm used to Kansas. See forty miles and sleep under the stars. When are we goin' to start fighting?" Albert Hazlett always chimed in with him, and the two fed each other's gloom.

One hot, sodden day, when the temperature in the attic must have been over one hundred and the walls were dripping wet, we were going through drill as usual. Brown had left Owen in charge of us, and Owen was giving us turns at commanding. At last my turn came. I fell out of ranks, took my place in front, and shouted, "Attention!"

Everyone jumped to the order but Bill Leeman. "Why can't we find some *men* for this company?" he sneered. "Damned if I'll take orders from you, girly." He threw down his rifle, yanked his coiled whip off his belt, and hit me across the face.

Instantly I was back on the riverfront in Cincinnati. I pitched into him as if he were one of Jacob's killers come back. "Here's a man's fight for you!" I shouted.

Leeman could have taken me apart if he'd known I was coming. But before he could react, one wild swing had found his nose and made it bleed. He fell back against Dauph Thompson and hit the floor. Then my hands were around his throat and he was on his back bucking like a wild colt and punching me, but I wouldn't be thrown off.

It must have lasted less than a minute. Then the others pulled us apart.

"You damned little Quaker devil," he said. "You broke my nose."

"No, he hasn't," Owen Brown said. "But it would have been fair enough if he had."

We stood glaring, ready to tear into each other again, and then—oh, glory! The thunder cracked right over our heads, and the rain began to pound on the roof like hail.

Dangerfield Newby looked out the little window. "You can't see the road!" he cried. "Come on." And we all ran whooping down the stairs out into the storm. The rain came sheeting down, hiding us as we shrieked and danced all over that hill. The thunder shook the ground, and the lightning scrawled across the sky.

Brown was furious when he heard about the fight. He made a long speech about Cain and Abel and brothers dwelling together in peace. Then he made Bill and me shake hands and apologize. We did, not meaning a word of it.

"I always say it never pays to get a Quaker mad," Newby murmured as we lay down that night.

"I'm not much of a Quaker," I said. "My mother is."

"Well, you fought like one," Newby said. "Took it serious. I think you'll have less trouble now. By the way, have you noticed anything about Leeman?"

"Only that he's a snake," I said.

"It's you and Barclay and Dauph that he rags on most," Newby said. "And they're the only two besides you who look younger than he does. And *you* really are younger."

"What are you saying?" I said.

"Just that Bill's young and scared. Probably more scared than we are. He wants to run, but he won't let himself. You and the others remind him of how young he is, and how frightened."

"You're not just saying that, are you?" I asked.

"Nope. Seems pretty clear to me," Newby said. "But then, he's fought before. He knows what the chances are better than we do."

"What do you think our chances are?" I asked.

Newby closed his eyes and shrugged. "Depends on what we try to do."

ELEVEN

Leeman backed off almost completely after our fight. He and Hazlett began sneaking out of the house late at night, hiding in the bushes until dawn. They almost never spoke, except to each other.

We speculated endlessly on what Brown's real plans were. Brown was in and out all the time on trips. I assumed he must be organizing the forces that would join us for the strike at Harper's Ferry. I knew he was sending a steady stream of letters to his son John Jr. about money and men. I knew several of us had been given commissions and offices in the government Brown meant to set up in the mountains. So things must be going forward. But I was impatient to get on with the business.

At last, one night in early September, Brown assembled us downstairs. Everyone was there, even Kagi and Cook. Brown unrolled a huge map of the slave states and spread it on the floor. It was marked with every arsenal and fort. A note on each state gave the number of slaves there. A tangle of arrows pointed every which way—into Virginia, the Carolinas, even Florida and Texas. But only one pointed north. It ran through the mountains above Harper's Ferry and stopped at the Canadian border.

"Men, the time is close," Brown said. "We must strike soon, and we shall. This is how it will be. We will seize the weapons at Harper's Ferry and spread the word to the slaves to meet us in the mountains west of here. We will establish a republic of free men, under the American flag. It will be a republic like those of the revolted slaves in Roman times. But this one will not be conquered. We will gain strength as runaways flock to join us. Those who cannot or will not fight with us, we will guide north to Canada.

"At first, we may have to retreat into the north from time to time. If we do, we will come back. And each time, we will come back stronger. Success will build on success. We will move farther south, and more slaves will rally to us. We will arm them from the arsenals in each state."

Brown stood back from the map and threw out an arm. "Under such an assault, slavery will collapse. The mere threat of our coming will cause the price of slaves to fall in every Southern state. Men will free their slaves for fear that they will free themselves, our way. I can't say how long it may take, perhaps years. But I hope and believe it will not be so long. One hard blow struck will shake the whole system, or even wreck it. Only strike that one blow and all the rest must follow."

Anderson nodded. Kagi crossed his arms. Stewart Taylor shouted, "Amen."

Then Dauph Thompson spoke up. "Captain, how many more men are coming, and when will they be here?"

"We are likely all," Brown said evenly.

No one spoke then. We looked at each other, looked at the floor. Unsaid words brooded between us.

Finally, Charlie Tidd ran his fingers through his beard and said, "This is the surest way to get us all killed. Damned if I'll throw my life away on this crackbrained scheme." Oliver and Owen Brown growled agreement.

Instantly we were all shouting at each other. We threw around words like "coward" and "madman" and got nowhere. Brown roared louder than anyone, and defended every comma in his plan. It wasn't long before we were split into two snarling camps. Charlie Tidd led one. Brown, of course, led the other. They were clustered on opposite sides of the room, with the two leaders doing most of the talking, while Kagi tried to bring them together.

I hesitated between them. Then I went to the door.

"Where are you going?" Annie said.

"Outside," I replied. "I'll be back soon."

Bill Leeman laughed.

I went as far away from the house as I could. There was a clump of trees up the rise behind the house, and a rock to sit on. The breeze sent the leaves sifting down around me. An owl cried, and another answered it. Light still hung over the western mountains, but the Big Dipper was out, its two guide stars pointing north, showing some runaway the road to freedom, if he could make it. I closed my eyes and tried to find the silent place within me.

My mind kept racing in circles like a frightened rabbit. Brown's plan was brilliant. Brown's plan could not work. I had to run. I had to fight. The sounds from the house rose and fell. I was in despair.

I was realizing for the first time the size of the thing

we meant to do. Slavery was the most powerful force in the United States of America. It selected our presidents and passed what laws it liked. Religions were set up to praise and defend its cruelties. Southern officers controlled the army, and held slaves while they did it.

What did we have? John Brown couldn't raise a thousand dollars at one time. And the only antislavery army on the planet was gathered in one room, at war with itself.

What do thee fear most?

I jumped. It was as though someone had spoken. "To die," I told the night.

Then thee should go home.

"But then I will be a coward," I said to myself.

Are thee sure?

"Yes," I answered.

Why do thee think so?

"Because of Jacob." It was the first thing that came into my head.

Jacob is dead. No one can hurt him now. And thee can do nothing for him.

"But I can do something for the others," I said.

Then thee have faith in Brown's plan?

"Yes," I said. "I don't know why. Maybe it's because it's the only plan there is. But I believe that, somehow, John Brown will free the slaves."

Then thee may choose. Go or stay. Brown will win with thee or without thee.

"Then I am free," I said.

Thee are as free as a man ever is.

Jacob's grave face came into my mind. I looked up at the sky again. The Dipper had wheeled a long way since

I sat down. It was time to go back. I walked up to the house, as free as a man ever is.

Owen Brown was sitting hunched over, bent under his father's eyes. The room was quiet.

"Thought you'd cut and run," Bill Leeman sneered.

I didn't answer him. I just went over and stood beside John Brown. Annie smiled. Brown nodded. Charlie Tidd shook his head.

For the next few days, we went through the motions of being a military company. More drill, more weapons cleaning, and more tense silence when a neighbor came by. But nothing was settled. Charlie and Owen and some of the others were talking about pulling out.

Finally, Brown called another meeting downstairs. It was dark outside, and only one lamp was lit in the big room on the ground floor. The sound of dishes being washed came in from the kitchen. It seemed odd at such a moment.

"Men," he said, "it may be that you are right, those of you who think my plan is not sound. I have decided to resign. I invite you all to choose another leader from among yourselves. Devise something better if you can."

Brown went back into the kitchen. Jeremiah Anderson rubbed his face and looked at the floor. Bill Leeman whispered a curse. Charlie Tidd spat his out loudly.

Then no one said anything, until Dangerfield Newby spoke: "Men, if you have another choice, make it now. Otherwise, come with me to Harper's Ferry," and he walked into the kitchen.

I followed. Shields Green, John Kagi, and Stewart Taylor were right behind me.

We found Brown bent over the table, scratching his pen across a sheet of cheap foolscap. Piles of paper surrounded the single smoking oil lamp. Martha was at the metal sink. Annie was standing behind her father, her big eyes full of fury.

"Captain," I said, "whatever you plan to do next, I want to be part of it."

"So do we all," Taylor announced.

Brown nodded. "Thank you. I seem to have no plan just now. We must await developments."

"Proceed as the way opens," I said. "That's the old Friends saying."

"Proceed as the way opens," he agreed. "I have always done that."

Annie slammed her fist against the wall. "It's a shame and disgrace on this country that there's only one man like Daddy," she said. "If there were a dozen, slavery wouldn't last a year. But there isn't. Every time Daddy leaves here, it's to go to someone who ought to help him but won't. Everywhere he goes, people pray and praise him and treat him like Moses. But will they come to fight? Not likely. You men are all. All in this country."

She put her head on Martha's shoulder and cried the way her father laughed—silently, her whole body shaking.

No one knew what to say. We had always thought Annie was dauntless. We wanted to comfort her but had no idea how.

At last Kagi spoke. "It can still work, even with so few," he assured us. "The essence of the plan is in speed, not numbers."

"If numbers told the tale, you Yankees would have conquered us Canadians in 1812," Taylor said.

"Mexicans had us outnumbered in every battle we had with 'em," Jeremiah Anderson agreed, joining us. "We won 'em all."

Brown put down his pen. "During the great uprising against the British in India two years ago, there was a Scotch parson and his family who were taken prisoner by the rebels," he said. "They were told that they would be killed the next morning. All night long the mother kept putting her ear to the ground and saying she could hear the war cry of a Scottish regiment growing louder and louder. 'Dinna ye hear it?' she kept asking her family. 'Dinna ye hear it?' They believed that she had gone mad, but they assured her that they heard it, too. The next morning when the sun rose, those rebels found their camp surrounded by that regiment. Somehow I feel that that story is for us."

"I hear it, Captain," Taylor said. "Before God, I do."

Annie dried her eyes on her apron. "Who wants tea and who wants coffee?"

We all had cups in hand when Owen Brown came into the room behind me, his shoulders more hunched than usual. He held a folded piece of paper in his hand. "Here, Father," he said, and left.

Brown read it. "It seems the doubters have decided to follow the old man after all. The way is opening."

Annie smiled broadly at her father. "I guess we all hear it, Daddy," she said.

Our doubts did not disappear. Some of us still mentioned leaving. But no one, not even Leeman or Hazlett, ever put a foot off the farm without Brown's permission. The Invisibles remained at full strength, such as it was.

October came, and turned gray. The rain fell cold. Our breaths began to hang in the air. Mold grew on the attic beams. We all were wound as tight as springs. Dauph Thompson started whistling the first notes of "Yankee Doodle" under his breath over and over. Newby took to suddenly punching at the air. Hazlett started wringing his hands. I spent every minute I could staring out our dirty little windows hoping for storms.

Then at last things began to happen. Brown sent Annie and Martha home. He moved most of our weapons to an old schoolhouse a few miles away and sent Owen there to guard them. He drilled us personally in the attic. In between drills, he wrote, wrote, wrote.

Nothing broke in on our concentration now. We worked with our rifles from the moment we woke up until we went to sleep, with only short breaks for a little food.

A few more men drifted in. The last to come was Francis Merriam from Boston. We heard he'd brought more than a thousand dollars with him to buy his place in the Invisibles. "He could have mine for nothing," Bill Leeman said. I wasn't certain he was joking.

Then a letter came from my mother. Most of the Invisibles got mail. It sounds surprising, but it is true. While we kept ourselves hidden, we were telling people all over the country more or less what we were up to. Letters came and went in big packets under the name of Isaac Smith. I never sent any, because I didn't want my family to find me. Now they had.

"How the Devil—" I muttered, tearing the envelope open. The letter was short, but my mother's careful writing told me that she had spent much time over it.

2nd October 1859

My Dearest Son,

I hope this letter may find thee well and in good spirits. We are all well here, but that we miss thee every moment. Thy sisters cannot understand where their brother has gone. Thy father hired a detective to try to find thee, but the man was a fool. He could no more find John Brown than a blind man could. Thy father told him he was sure thee were wherever Brown was, and the man went to the Brown farm, but learned nothing and got no farther.

I have found thee, as I hope, by my own methods. John Brown is not hard to find if one wants to do so. Julia Howe has always been a great friend to me.

Theodore, I do not beg thee to return, though I wish it with all my heart. I know what thee are doing, and, while I can never approve of violence, I must believe thee are proceeding by the light thee have been given. So long as thee do so, I trust thee will be under God's wing.

Could thee not write to me just to let me know that thee are well? I swear I will tell no one, not even thy father, if thee do. But it will ease my heart beyond telling if thee will do only that much.

Bless Thee, My Son,
Thy Mother, Caroline Evans Worth

I felt a rush of shame at worrying my family, and of gratitude toward my mother. I borrowed a pencil from Stewart Taylor and wrote back at once.

October 14th, 1859

My Dearest Mother,

You letter has just arrived. I am well and safe. The others here are good fellows. I wish you could meet them. If you did, I know you would be less worried. Many of them have done this kind of work before and know what they are about. We seem to have everything we need to make a good beginning.

I am glad that you know what I am doing. I am sorry to worry you so much. Thank you for keeping what you know secret. I think you will not have to do so much longer. We have been here so long that either we must do something or give it up, at least for now.

Give my best regards to Mrs. Howe.

Your Son,
Theodore

I looked at what I had written. Nothing in it was untrue, but the letter was one lie from start to finish. I took another sheet of paper and wrote the truth.

October 14th, 1859

Dearest Mother,

Thank you for not telling what you know or trying to get me back. I couldn't stand the shame of leaving, even though I expect I will never see any of you again.

*We have been here so long that something must happen
soon or the men here will start to leave. Brown seems
to be trying hard to make a beginning, but there are
so many obstacles and so little support, it is a wonder
he has got this far. I do not see how we can succeed.
Still, he must do something or fail completely. I cannot
imagine that he would accept that. He would ride into
Harper's Ferry all alone rather than do nothing now.*

*I will write you again if there is time before we
launch our attack. If not, this letter will likely be the
last word you ever have from me. Please know that I
always loved you.*

> *Your Son,*
> *Theodore*

I read both letters over. Then I folded the first one
and put it into the big envelope Brown had left for our
mail. I looked again at the other and tore it up.

On the night of October fifteenth, John Brown swore us
in as citizens of his provisional republic. Those of us who
were to be army officers received commissions signed
by Kagi.

Since I wasn't one of them, I went to get my gear
ready. The attic was empty for once. Everyone else was
downstairs watching the swearing-in of the officers. The
place looked sad and dirty now. It seemed as though I
had been there forever. Now I was looking at it for the
last time. Whatever happened, I would never see it again.

I cleaned the breech and barrel of my Sharps. I slipped
my cartridge box over my head and made sure it held

forty rounds. I hung a bayonet on my belt. I was as ready as I would ever be.

Steps came up the stairs behind me.

"Worth. I missed you downstairs," Brown said.

"I'm anxious to get on with it," I replied.

"So am I," Brown said. "Well, all is going forward now. I'm sending a few of the boys to Colonel Washington's plantation to fetch him and a sword I want. George Washington's sword. It's going to the mountains with us. Owen is at the schoolhouse. The rest of us are heading down to the arsenal in about an hour."

I nodded.

"Worth, I want you to put up your rifle. I've a particular plan for you."

I wasn't sure I had heard him right. "Put up my rifle?" I said. "Where?"

"It doesn't matter," Brown said.

A thought flashed through my mind. "You're not going to leave me behind?"

"No," said Brown. "It's rather different from that. I'm sending you off with your telegraph. I want you to roam up and down the wires, listening in. I reckon that the news of what we're going to do at Harper's Ferry will get out sometime tomorrow. When it does, I want you to pass the messages on to me if you can. I want you, too, to send false messages to confuse our enemies. That will buy us time and help us to know which route to take out of town. It's a job only you can do, and it could make the difference between success and failure for us."

"But Captain, who can read any messages I send you?"

"Oh, Kagi knows the Morse," Brown said. "I expect

he didn't tell you. You will send me messages through him."

I didn't know what to say or what I felt. Relief? Yes, and guilt. And anger. "Captain Brown," I stammered, "I'm as much a member of this company as any man, and I have a right to go into battle with it."

"There'll be plenty of battles later, Worth," Brown snapped. "Slavery won't fall at the first tap we give it, you know; never mind what I said before. Mind me now; after we get away, you'll know about it from the wires. And you'll be able to calculate where we've gone. You'll join us in the mountains, and there you'll likely get all the fighting you want."

"You're not doing this because I'm the youngest man here, are you, Captain?" I said.

"You aren't young anymore," Brown said. "You have not been young since Cincinnati. I would not have brought you if you were."

"What about my rifle?" I asked.

"You won't need it tomorrow," Brown said. "Take this instead, for emergencies." He handed me the little pistol he carried in his pants. I slid it behind my belt.

"I'll need a horse," I said.

"Take whichever one you like best," Brown said.

"When do I leave?" I asked.

"Now," Brown said. "I want you down on the Baltimore & Ohio line as quick as you can get there."

My telegraph was sitting by the head of my mattress. I slung it over my shoulder and put on my hat.

Brown stuck out his hand. "Good-bye, Worth," he said. "We'll make a good fight."

"I'm sure we will, Captain."

I went downstairs. The house was empty. Everyone was in the barn. Kagi was supervising the loading of the wagon they would take with them to Harper's Ferry. John Cook and Dangerfield Newby were sliding a crate of Sharps rifles onto the tailgate.

"Here you are," Dauph Thompson said. "Bear a hand with these pikes."

"Can't," I said. "The captain's sending me off to fiddle with the telegraph."

"Oh, well, so long for now, then," Thompson said.

Since I was no horseman, I threw a blanket and saddle on Frank, the only horse I'd ever ridden before, and led him outside. The night was cloudy, cold, and moonless. Rain was getting ready to fall. I reckoned I would be soaked by morning. I turned and waved into the dark barn. One pale hand waved back. I didn't know whose it was.

"I'll see you in the mountains," I said.

There was no answer. I rode away, and the fog took me in.

TWELVE

I rode almost three miles before I found the spot that I wanted. The trees were thick, and the wires hung conveniently low. It was as good a place as I was going to get.

I tethered Frank. Carefully, I climbed the nearest pole and connected to the wires. The wet made them spark fiercely. I listened. There was no traffic on the line. I hung there and got slowly soaked. After about an hour, I tried sending Kagi a short message. No answer came. I worried if the wet had shorted out the wire to Harper's Ferry. Not likely, but a cracked insulator could have leaked.

I wondered if everything had gone according to plan. It crossed my mind that if, for any reason, the raid was postponed, there would be no way to get word to me. That would be a joke. I might be the only Invisible to go into action. I didn't believe it could happen, but it made me laugh.

Then, as the clouds in the east began to turn from black to gray, the wire leapt to life:

```
     TO PRESIDENT, BALTIMORE & OHIO RAILROAD
     SIR STOP ABOLITIONISTS LED BY JOHN BROWN
   HAVE SEIZED THE TOWN AND ARSENAL AT
   HARPER'S FERRY STOP THEY HELD UP THIS TRAIN
   ABOUT FOUR HOURS STOP TELEGRAPH TO
   HARPER'S FERRY CUT STOP ADVISE GOVERNOR
   WISE AT ONCE TO SEND MILITIA STOP
   SIGNED CONDUCTOR TRAIN 42
```

So it had begun. Brown must have cut the wires for some reason and detained the train until he was ready to escape with the weapons. He must be on his way to the mountains by now. Our war was under way. I wondered if I should leave my perch now and start looking for the Invisibles or wait a while.

"I haven't done any mischief yet," I said quietly to myself. I sent another message:

```
   OSAWATOMIE BROWN AT HARPER'S FERRY
   WITH SEVEN HUNDRED MEN STOP ARSENAL
   SEIZED STOP OTHER ABOLITIONIST ATTACKS
   EXPECTED IN AREA STOP FOR GOD'S SAKE
```

I left the message unfinished.

That seemed to stir things up. It wasn't long before I heard:

```
     COMMANDING GENERAL MARYLAND FIRST
   LIGHT DIVISION NOTIFIED STOP PRESIDENT
   BUCHANAN NOTIFIED STOP HELP IS COMING
   STOP BE RESOLUTE
   SIGNED GOVERNOR HENRY A. WISE
```

I wondered who the governor intended the message for. Anyway, I sent him a reply: BROWN NOW BELIEVED

TO HAVE AS MANY AS FIFTEEN HUNDRED MEN STOP, and didn't sign it. Then I sent:

> GOVERNOR HENRY A. WISE
> ABOLITIONIST FORCES ESTIMATED AT TEN
> THOUSAND BELIEVED EN ROUTE TO
> WASHINGTON CITY STOP COULD YOU NOT
> REDIRECT FIRST LIGHT DIVISION TO DEFENSE OF
> THE CAPITAL STOP
> SIGNED JAMES BUCHANAN, PRESIDENT OF THE
> UNITED STATES

This had a wonderful effect:

> PRESIDENT JAMES BUCHANAN
> SIR STOP FIRST LIGHT DIVISION NOT
> AVAILABLE FOR FEDERAL SERVICE STOP WILL
> RALLY TO YOU AS SOON AS POSSIBLE STOP
> GOVERNOR HENRY A. WISE

And after a while:

> GOVERNOR HENRY A. WISE
> FIRST LIGHT DIVISION NOT REQUIRED HERE
> STOP PLEASE ADVISE CONCERNING REPORTS OF
> ABOLITIONIST REBELS STOP
> PRESIDENT JAMES BUCHANAN

It kept getting better. Other towns in Maryland and Virginia were seeing abolitionists in the bushes. I read their messages and improved where I could:

> PRESIDENT JAMES BUCHANAN
> SIR STOP ABOLITIONISTS BELIEVED HEADED
> FOR CAPITAL NOW KNOWN TO BE ADVANCING TO
> RICHMOND STOP SEND REINFORCEMENTS OR

Which brought:

> GOVERNOR HENRY A. WISE
> TROOPS ARE NOT AVAILABLE HERE STOP GOD
> BLESS YOU IN THIS HOUR OF CRISIS STOP
> PRESIDENT JAMES BUCHANAN

I was beginning to enjoy my correspondence with the White House:

> PRESIDENT JAMES BUCHANAN
> WE WILL SELL OURSELVES AS DEARLY AS
> POSSIBLE BUT I FEAR THIS MAY AFFECT YOUR
> CHANCES OF REELECTION STOP
> GOVERNOR HENRY A. WISE

Then came:

> ALL OPERATORS AND STATIONMASTERS
> NOT ALL MESSAGES ON THIS LINE ARE TO BE
> BELIEVED STOP ABOLITIONIST RAIDERS MAY BE
> SENDING FALSE WARNINGS STOP REFER ALL
> MESSAGES TO THIS OFFICE FOR VERIFICATION
> STOP
> GOVERNOR HENRY A. WISE

It looked as though my game was nearly up, but I would wait a little longer. I might hear something good to take to my friends in the mountains, something we could laugh at tonight.

The next message was:

> BROWN SURROUNDED NOW IN ARSENAL
> BUILDINGS STOP MILITIA HERE HAVE SITUATION

IN HAND BUT DECLINE TO STORM STRONG
POINTS STOP SEND REINFORCEMENTS AT ONCE
STOP
SIGNED JOHN D. STARRY MD

Militia? My stomach turned over. But there were no militia around Harper's Ferry. Was someone else playing tricks on the wires? The Invisibles had got away into the mountains hours ago.

After a while, another message clacked through:

MARINES UNDER COLONEL ROBERT LEE EN
ROUTE FROM WASHINGTON CITY STOP EXPECT
THEM BY TONIGHT STOP
SIGNED GOVERNOR HENRY A. WISE

The Washington marines. If the Invisibles *were* still at Harper's Ferry, if they *were* surrounded by militia, that militia could only be a scratch force of volunteers with hunting weapons and no training. We could probably fight our way through men like that. The marines were another matter entirely. If we were still in Harper's Ferry by nightfall, we would never get out.

I sent another message:

GOVERNOR HENRY A. WISE
SIR STOP WE HAVE REPORTS THAT JOHN
BROWN IS TRAPPED AT HARPER'S FERRY AND
THAT MARINES ARE GOING THERE STOP CAN YOU
VERIFY STOP
CAPTAIN JOHN H. KAGI

The answer came back quickly:

TO ALL ON THIS LINE
RUMORS THAT JOHN BROWN IS SURROUNDED
AT HARPER'S FERRY ARE TRUE STOP FEDERAL
MARINES EXPECTED THERE BY TONIGHT STOP
GOVERNOR HENRY A. WISE

How could Brown, Osawatomie Brown, have been so stupid? He was an old guerrilla fighter; he knew he had to have his retreat planned out. But it had happened. There was no reason to hope for him, or anyone with him. And if anyone suspected I had been with him, I was as good as dead. The best thing for me to do now was to get north as fast as I could.

And yet, I was an Invisible. I couldn't leave without knowing for certain what had happened. So, against all common sense, I rode back toward Harper's Ferry.

I could hear wild tides of noise coming from the town as I neared it. A chant rose and fell in the midst of the babble, but I couldn't quite make out the words. When I reached the middle of the bridge across the Potomac, I stopped and looked down. Something was waving at me.

It was Bill Leeman. He was bent nearly double against the piling. His body was pocked with bullet holes, and half his head had been shot away. His one eye was turned up in what was left of his face. His upstream arm was cocked over his head. His hand floated limply in the swift current. He looked as though he were still trying to run.

I went cold. I got down and held on to the railing to steady myself. This was nothing like my grandfather's death. "Oh, Bill" was all I could say. "Oh, Bill."

If there had been one of us whom I would have wanted dead, it would have been him. But all I felt was pity, horror, and a kind of loyalty.

As I neared the end of the bridge, I saw another body floating face up at the edge of the water. It was what was left of Bill Thompson. His face was hideous.

I could hear the chanting clearly now. "Kill them, kill them, kill them, kill them" was coming from hundreds of throats. Newly minted militia men were waving their weapons drunkenly.

As I turned down the street that led to the armory, a ragged double file of men approached me. The man at the head of the column ordered it to halt and came over to me with his pistol out.

"Who might you be?" he demanded.

I forced myself to look straight into his face. It was the leader of the slave catchers we had encountered that day above Harper's Ferry. I said the first thing that came into my head.

"Name's Bob Gibbons. Telegrapher. Looking for work. What's going on?"

"You talk like a Yankee," he said.

"I am," I said. "Is there a crime in that?"

"There might be," he said. "There just might be."

Then a voice behind him called out, "Hey, Cap Brannan, ain't he one of them we saw up in the mountains that day? Back when we was slave-catchin' them two last summer?"

"Who's that, another one?" some of them called out. "We'll finish him now."

"My name's Bob Gibbons. I'm a telegrapher. I'm looking for work," I said.

Frank and I were surrounded by drunken men with rifles. Somebody grabbed Frank's bridle. Another man cupped his hands under my stirrup and threw me to the ground.

I got to my feet. "What is all this?" I said. "Isn't there anybody here who can tell me what's going on?"

"Oh, there's a lot goin' on," someone shouted. "He look familiar to you?"

I was shoved along the street until we came to a body lying in the gutter. It had been shot through the throat and torn by animals. Its ears were cut off. Dangerfield Newby.

"Oh, my God," I said.

"Put up your hands," Brannan ordered.

I did. He yanked my little pistol out of my belt and smelled the barrel. "Ain't been fired," he said. Then added, "Lately." He called over his shoulder, "Corporal Wallace."

A little man with a potbelly came over and tried to salute.

"Corporal, you are to escort this here prisoner back to Harper's Ferry and put him with the others," he said. "Take two men with you. If he tries to escape, shoot the Yankee bastard in the back."

"Aw, Captain, I want to go up to Pleasant Valley with you," the new corporal said.

"Follow your orders, Corporal," Brannan said, waving his pistol at him.

Corporal Wallace shrugged and called to two men who were as reluctant as he was to return to town. Brannan swung up onto Frank.

"Hey," I said. "That's my horse."

Brannan laughed. "I requisition this horse in the name of Brannan's Company, Maryland Militia," he said. "You can have him back when the war's over. If you ain't hanged first." And that was the last I ever saw of Frank.

They hustled me along down the street a short distance. Then a new knot of drunks surrounded us.

"Who's that? Is he one of them? We'll string him up," they shouted.

"My name's Bob Gibbons," I said. "I'm a telegrapher looking for work."

"The only work for your kind is rope stretchin'," someone shouted. "Give him to us."

"If we let 'em have him, we can still catch up with the company, Corp," one of my guards said.

"You're thinking good today, Randall," the corporal said.

In seconds, I was lifted off my feet and passed along to a building with a high-roofed porch. I felt a rope around my neck.

Then there was a tall, handsome man in a blue uniform in front of me. He had a squad of marines with him.

"Gentlemen," he said, "I accept this prisoner from you in the name of the United States." And he lifted the noose off me.

"Kill him, kill him, kill him," the chant started. But the man who had rescued me silenced it with a look. "There has been enough killing," he said. "Sergeant, convey this prisoner to the engine house."

The marine sergeant snapped a salute, and the militia parted for us like water.

The officer walked along beside us. His uniform told me that he was a full colonel. He must have been the man who led the troops that overcame us.

"Sir, I'm just a telegrapher," I said. "My name's Bob Gibbons, I came down from the North looking for work. I don't know anything about what's going on here. I've had my horse stolen and nearly been lynched. Please, let me go."

The colonel smiled gently under his fine moustache. "I'm afraid that won't be possible, sir. At present, Harper's Ferry is under martial law. And under my command. I fear I must hold you, at least for the moment. In any case, it hardly seems safe to release you just now, even if what you tell me is true. Believe me when I say that I regret this sorry necessity. This is a terrible day for our country."

We had reached the engine house. A ring of marines stood guard around it. A line of bodies lay along one wall, with their faces covered.

"But I haven't done anything wrong," I said.

"I fear that may be said of many who have died here," the colonel said. "Believe me, I will do my best for you. But the civil authorities must hear your case."

"What case?" I said.

The colonel led me to the door of a small attached building. The marines there came to present arms. "There has been an abolitionist raid on the arsenal here," he said. "Numbers are dead on both sides. We expect more trouble. But here comes a sheriff to take charge of you." He saluted me. "I regret your trouble, sir," he said, then turned on his heel and left.

"In here with you," the sheriff said. "I reckon you know most of these fellows well enough."

Shields Green raised his head from his hands, looked at me, and said, "Who's that?"

"What are you putting him in here for?" Edwin Coppoc demanded.

There was a body lying on the floor at the back of the room. A head turned slowly toward me. "Who are you, boy?" Watson Brown groaned.

They were trying to save me. "I'm supposed to be an abolitionist raider," I said.

"Let him go, sheriff," Watson said slowly. "We came here to free slaves, not to rob cradles."

The sheriff locked the door.

I sat between Shields and Edwin and held their hands. I knew now why I had come back. There were no words for how I felt. Live or die, I was one of these men.

When I could trust myself to talk, I whispered, "Are we all?"

"Don't know," Edwin said. "A few may have got away. But I know John Jr.'s dead. So are Taylor, Dauphin, and Jeremiah Anderson. The captain's wounded—badly. I don't know about the others. We weren't all in the engine house."

"I saw Bill Leeman's body in the river," I said. "And Bill Thompson's. Newby's lying in the street. He looked like something had eaten him."

Watson groaned terribly, and Shields Green looked up. "That's hard," he said. "All us good men, and the bad ones thundering right over us."

"Thanks for lying for me," I said.

"We'll do it again if we get the chance," Edwin said.

"I tried to get away myself," Shields said. "When they broke into the engine house, I got rid of my gun and bullets. Said I'd been a prisoner of the old man. But the real prisoners all told on me. Ain't no disgrace not to want to die."

"If they do let you go, you can tell our story," Edwin said to me. "It would be something not to be forgotten."

Watson spoke. "My heart tells me you will live," he said. "You will live for all of us." He licked his lips. "Do we have any water?"

We didn't. I went to the door and knocked. After a while, it cracked open. I looked into the face of a marine over his bayoneted rifle. "We have a dying man in here," I said. "Can we get some water?"

"He can get a drink in Hell when he gets there," the marine said, and the door slammed.

We sat listening to Watson dying all night long. The next day, someone brought him one cup of water and lifted him up onto a bench when he asked for it.

Later that day, they marched us all under heavy guard to the train heading eight miles down the track to Charlestown.

When I got onto the car, I saw John Brown lying in the aisle on a stretcher. Watson was lying at his feet. Aaron Stevens was next. Besides Brown and Stevens, the only survivor I hadn't already seen was John Copeland. He was sitting next to Stevens.

"They got me when we tried to make a break from the rifle works," he told me later. "Kagi and Leary were with me. None of us made it."

If Brown recognized me, my chance of being released

was gone. But he seemed not to recognize any of us just then. In spite of the heavy jolting of the train, he was almost asleep. Only when we hit a hard bump or went around a sharp curve did he say anything, and then it made no sense.

Charlestown had a strong county jail. They kept us there under heavy guard. The marines and the handsome colonel were gone. We were Virginian property now. I shared a cell with Watson for a little while. Then he died and I was alone.

Brown came back to himself later that day. He looked at me through the bars that divided our cells and said, "So, Worth, I thought you had got away."

"Beg your pardon, mister," I said, "but my name is Gibbons. Bob Gibbons. I'm a telegrapher."

"I see," he said.

There was a guard in front of each cell, so at least two men had heard us. I felt my last hope go.

I sat waiting for what would happen next. When two men in fine suits came to examine me that afternoon, it was almost a relief.

"I am Mayor Charles C. Green," the older one introduced himself. "This is Judge Richard Parker. We apologize for not having come to see you sooner."

"How do you do, gentlemen," I said. "My name is Bob Gibbons."

"So we have been given to understand," Judge Parker said. "And that is what we are here to ascertain. Your case is an unusual one. You may or may not be who you say you are. You may or may not be an abolitionist raider. At present there are no charges framed against you at all. Perhaps there should not be. You may be an innocent victim of circumstance. On the other hand, one of my bailiffs informs me that today, in his hearing, John Brown addressed you as 'Worth' and said that he thought you had got away."

"That's right, your honor," I said. "And I told him, I'm Bob Gibbons, just like I'm telling you."

From his cot, Brown said, "There was a man named Worth with us. I do not know what happened to him. When I saw that young man there, I thought at first he was Worth. Then my head cleared and I saw I was wrong."

"Have you any identification at all?" Judge Parker asked.

"Only my word and my telegraph key," I said.

"Hardly conclusive," said Mayor Green.

Judge Parker looked through a thin sheaf of papers. "I have a communication here from the officer who took you in charge that you were recognized upon the bridge at Harper's Ferry by himself and another man as one who had been seen in the company of Brown several weeks previously. Can you account for your whereabouts in the last months?"

"That would be the man who stole my horse," I said.

Judge Parker raised his eyebrows. "Horse?"

"I had a horse named Frank and he stole it," I said. "Maybe if I were a horse thief, I'd want people to think the man I'd robbed was a criminal, too."

Judge Parker put his hand to his eyes. "This case is vexing," he said. "I have men who must be put on trial for treason and murder. I do not have time just now to deal with horse thievery as well. Surely there must be some way to determine your identity."

"Who was your last employer?" the mayor asked.

"The Western of Boston," I said.

"You are a very long way from Boston," the judge said.

I shrugged. "I like to travel."

"I believe the thing to do is to contact the Western of Boston and inquire of them," the judge said. "Who was your superior there?"

I thought fast. "Mr. Webster."

"First name?"

"He was always 'Mr. Webster' to me."

"I shall send a message with your physical description and the particulars of your circumstances today," the mayor said. "If you are who you say, to hold you any longer is a flagrant miscarriage of justice."

"That will be all for now, I think," the judge said. "We shall return either to release you or to charge you properly."

There was a small rectangle of sunlight on the floor of my cell. I made a great study of it for the rest of the day. I watched closely as it changed shape, moved across to the wall, and at last disappeared.

My mind kept dancing in a mad circle that wouldn't stop. Would Bob be in his office? Would he remember our code that we had never used? Would he recall me naming him Webster that day in the bar? Would he still be working for the Western of Boston? And would he help me if he could?

It was long past dark when the door down at the end of the line of cells opened again. The mayor, a bailiff, and a man I hadn't seen before were there. The mayor had a jaunty new bounce in his step.

"This is the one," he said.

The bailiff came into the cell and clapped irons on my wrists.

"Come along," he said.

They led me out the door and into a courtroom. Judge Parker was there. "Well, you have led us on a merry chase," he said. "And it is very late. But we Southerners love the chase. Mr. Harding, show the prisoner the evidence against him."

The man I didn't know turned to me. "Permit me," he said. "I am Charles B. Harding, county attorney. It is my duty to acquaint you with the evidence against you."

"All right," I said. "Whatever I did, I did for reasons that seemed good to me and still do. Do what you have to."

He shoved a telegram under my nose. I felt my jaw drop as I read it.

HONORABLE CHARLES C. GREEN
THE MAN YOU HOLD ROBERT GIBBONS IS
WANTED BY US IN THE MATTER OF THE
EMBEZZLEMENT OF TWO THOUSAND DOLLARS
STOP CHARGE HIM AND HOLD HIM UNTIL WE CAN
COLLECT HIM STOP WE ARE COMING AT ONCE
STOP
SIGNED NICHOLAS WEBSTER, VICE-PRESIDENT,
WESTERN OF BOSTON RR

"Small wonder you like to travel, Mr. Gibbons," Mayor Green said. "But I fear your next journey will be back to your old haunts."

I stood with my head hanging and tears of joy falling

onto the courtroom floor while they formally charged me with being an embezzler, and being Bob Gibbons.

I had three days to wait for my deliverance. In that time, two more of the Invisibles were brought in. John Cook and Albert Hazlett had both been taken in Pennsylvania, where they had thought they were safe. They were at the opposite end of the line of cells from me, so I saw them only once. "Hello again" was all Cook said.

On the third day, the guard on us was lifted somewhat. Just two bailiffs were kept in the block. It gave me my last chance to speak to John Brown.

I sat on my bunk as close to him as I could. I kept my hands folded and my face down. I looked, I hoped, like a very guilty man. He was still lying on his bed.

"Captain Brown, what went wrong?" I murmured when the afternoon had made the guards a little drowsy.

"Everything, maybe. Or maybe nothing," Brown answered. "It is not over yet. Everything that happens now has been ordained. Or so I believe."

"You mean you never meant to leave Harper's Ferry at all?" I said.

"I meant to begin what has begun," he said. "The means are not so important." He turned on his side a little. "Let me tell you what happened in that engine house. I had everything I wanted in there. Even Washington's sword. Washington's sword in my hand. I had pushed the fire engine against the doors, and it gave them a devil of a time breaking in. They used a ladder as a battering ram. They opened a small hole in the bottom and started to crawl through. That was hot work. But then the doors fell back against the engine, and they swarmed up and over. They used their bayonets on us.

"Their officer saw me and jumped down on me from the fire engine. He tried to stab me with his sword. But he'd brought the wrong one, Worth. It was his shiny little dress sword, not a real blade. Still, he might have finished me with it. But he stabbed me in the breastbone, right where my two leather cartridge belts crossed. His blade bent. All he could do was beat me with the hilt. God has taken the sword into His hand now. I have been spared for the work to come."

Even so, Brown had very nearly died of those blows.

"Spared?" I said. "But what can you do now?"

"I can proceed as the way opens," Brown said.

"But what about me? Did you mean to—" I began.

"Look, Worth," Brown said, "it is no good brooding about the past. Especially not for you. We must go forward. All of us. By different ways. Now I am tired. Goodbye, if I am asleep when you leave." And he turned away from me.

Later that night, the bailiffs came and led me out. I looked back over my shoulder, but the cells were all dark. My friends were truly invisible now.

They took me back into the courtroom. There were three men waiting for me. One was a giant in a loud suit flourishing a pair of handcuffs and some papers. He almost hid Bob Gibbons from sight.

When I came into the room, Bob whirled around and shouted, "That's him! He's the one who did it. See, Mr. Webster, I told you we'd run him down sooner or later."

"Indeed. You were right, Worth. I never should have doubted you," my father said.

Mayor Green smiled. "I took the liberty of informing this gentleman that you had already confessed."

"Though with the evidence this faithful employee has provided me, your admission is hardly necessary," Father said, and he clapped Bob on the shoulder. To me he said, "It's back to Massachusetts for you."

I was signed out of the jail and into the custody of the detective my father had brought. He slapped the handcuffs on me and led me out.

"I must advise you to say nothing more concerning your case," my father said. "You are in trouble enough."

"Wait till we're on a train headin' north," Bob muttered.

There was a carriage waiting for us. The detective drove us north as fast as he could. The road took us through Harper's Ferry. It was quiet tonight, just as it must have been the night John Brown came into it to—do what? Start a war? Split the nation? Offer himself up to his fierce God? To free the slaves?

Yes, that was for certain if nothing else was. To free the slaves.

The Potomac rolled dark below us as we rattled across the bridge to Baltimore.

AFTERWARDS

 They hanged John Brown on a hill near Harper's Ferry with three thousand militia surrounding his scaffold. All for one old man with his hands tied and a noose around his neck.

It was a windy, bitter day when his body came home. About twenty of us were waiting for it. I helped to dig the grave under the huge rock carved with his name. The clouds went racing south like an army of ghosts.

I was the only one of the Invisibles there. Most of us, of course, were dead, or waiting to be hanged. A few, like me, had got away and were in hiding. I did not need to hide, since I had never come near the battle or fired a shot. Officially, I had never been there. I was the most invisible of us all.

The women were a terrible sight. Martha hung on Mrs. Brown as if every bone in her body were broken. Mrs. Brown was quiet until we lowered the coffin into the ground and started to throw dirt on it. Then she howled. But Annie frightened me the most. She stared straight into the grave without trying to wipe away her tears, and smiled.

Afterwards, she came over to me and took my hand.

"I'm glad you could be here," she said. "It's right that one of you should see the beginning."

"Thank you, Annie" was all I said, wondering what she was talking about. But she was right. It was the beginning. Just as he had at Osawatomie Creek, John Brown had forced every man to choose his side.

The Harper's Ferry raid shook the cage where the South kept its deepest fears locked up. Almost a year to the day after John Brown was executed, South Carolina seceded from the Union. Six more Southern states joined her. No one in the North knew what to do. Then, in April of '61, the South fired on the American flag flying over Fort Sumter, and we knew. We marched away to our training camps, singing,

> *John Brown's body lies a-mold'ring in the grave,*
> *John Brown's body lies a-mold'ring in the grave,*
> *John Brown's body lies a-mold'ring in the grave,*
> *But his soul goes marching on.*

I left Harvard and volunteered as an army telegrapher. Bob came with me.

"If the army's hard up enough to take you, then I'd better come along to keep an eye on your work," he said.

We get less pay than soldiers, and every once in a while somebody shoots at us, but whatever comes over the wires, we're first to know it. Makes us feel spry.

We sing a new song now. One Julia Ward Howe wrote because she loved John Brown and thought the words we had did him no justice.

> *Mine eyes have seen the glory*
> *Of the coming of the Lord,*

> *He is tramping out the vintage*
> *Where the grapes of wrath are stored,*
> *He has loosed the fateful lightning*
> *Of his terrible swift sword,*
> *His truth is marching on.*

She is right. Brown wrote his name, and our fate, in lightning.

There is so much I still don't know. I will never know if Brown meant to stage his raid as he explained it to us or if he intended to sacrifice himself and us to bring on this war. I know now that he cut the wires to Harper's Ferry before he even reached it. He held up a train for hours, then identified himself and let it go on to Baltimore. He let a man from Harper's Ferry gallop off to spread the alarm. What was in his mind?

I will never know if he intended for me to live. I asked my mother point-blank if she had given Brown money to buy me a chance to get away. "There is not enough money in all the world to buy thee, Theodore" was all she said.

My friends from the Invisibles are close to me in a way I can't explain. I try to live for us all, as Watson said I would. I never feel John Brown. Wherever he is, it seems a long way from here. Oddly, though, I sometimes wake up dreaming that I have heard him. It is always the same dream, a dream that makes no sense. I hear him singing in his flat, hard voice the song I heard on the docks at Cincinnati the day that Jacob died. It is soft but persistent, and absolutely real.

> *Deep river,*
> *My home is over Jordan,*

> *Deep river, Lord,*
> *I want to cross over into campground,*
> *I want to cross over into campground.*

John Brown may have his peace. We have his war.

THE RAIDERS

Jeremiah Anderson *Killed in action*
Osborne Perry Anderson *Survived; fought in Civil War*
John Brown, Jr. *Killed in action*
Oliver Brown *Killed in action*
Owen Brown *Survived*
Watson Brown *Died in prison from wounds received in action*
John Cook *Escaped Harper's Ferry; caught later, tried, and hanged*
John Copeland *Hanged*
Barclay Coppoc *Survived raid; died in Civil War*
Edwin Coppoc *Hanged*
Shields Green *Hanged*
Albert Hazlett *Escaped Harper's Ferry; caught later, tried, and hanged*
John Henry Kagi *Killed in action*
Lewis Leary *Killed in action*
William Leeman *Killed in action*
Francis Merriam *Survived; fought in Civil War*
Dangerfield Newby *Killed in action*
Aaron Stevens *Hanged*
Stewart Taylor *Killed in action*
Charles Tidd *Escaped*
Dauphin Thompson *Killed in action*
William Thompson *Taken prisoner and shot*

John Brown *Hanged*

Theodore Worth, his family, and Bob Gibbons are ficti-
tious characters. The rest of *Lightning Time* is as accurate
as I could make it. The Reverend Mr. Howe and Mr.
Sanborn were part of a group called the Secret Six, which
also included Gerrit Smith, reputed to be the richest man
in America; the Reverend Thomas Wentworth Higginson,
who led one of the first African-American regiments in the
Civil War; the Reverend Theodore Parker; and Charles
Henry Parkhurst. They were devoted to destroying either
slavery or the union of the Northern with the Southern
states. Had Brown wished to do so, he could have impli-
cated them sufficiently to have them tried for treason.
They nearly were, anyway.

Besides the Invisibles known to us by name, there
were a few others, apparently all African-Americans, who
passed through the Kennedy farm and either left or were
waiting nearby to see if Brown succeeded at Harper's
Ferry. If he had gone into the mountains as he intended,
he might have rallied the support he hoped for. In any
case, adding one young white man to the short list of
those whose names have not come down to us does not
go far beyond the bounds of history.

It is also true that there were false messages jumping
up and down the wires during and just after the Harper's

Ferry raid. The mysterious request for assistance in repelling an attack on Pleasant Valley was real. Robert E. Lee and twenty-five marines marched off to defend the town but found no trouble there. Possibly someone like Theodore was at work.

Brown's trial, as Theodore indicates, was a solemn farce. The charge, treason against Virginia, was meaningless. Aside from the question of whether treason against a state is possible, Brown was not a Virginian and had never lived there. His attack was on a U.S. government arsenal. If he had committed treason, it was against the United States, but President Buchanan was afraid to try him for it.

John Brown's execution was attended by three thousand militia and cadets from the Virginia Military Institute. One of the militiamen was a young actor named John Wilkes Booth. One of the commanders of the cadets was a former U.S. Army major named Thomas J. Jackson. Within two years of Brown's death, Major Jackson would lead Confederate troops to more victories than all other Southern generals combined and become known to history as Stonewall. Booth would assassinate Abraham Lincoln.

The Fugitive Slave Law, the Kansas-Nebraska Act, and the Under Ground Rail Road (as it was written in Theodore's time) are part of American history, as are Dangerfield Newby's life story, the suicide season in northern Virginia, and John Brown's lonely struggle against slavery.